SARAH KAMINSKI

My Mother's Daughter

To Oliver and Benjamin, my children.
My life would not be complete without you.

New Moon

The smell of chlorine and sunscreen lingers in the air, which is heavy with humidity and anticipation. Between the warmth of Jeremiah's body pressed against mine and the sunshine seeping in through my open window, there's a glow in the air. Or maybe it's him and this moment right now.

I draw in a shallow breath and glance up at him. Gold-flecked eyes meet mine, their expression happy and soft, but it quickly turns to concern.

"I'm not hurting you, am I?" he asks, pausing. His weight shifts on top of me, and for a second, I worry he'll pull away.

I shake my head. "I'm fine." Fine. Great. So happy. He's definitely not hurting me.

He smiles and kisses me. A long, slow kiss. My lips part and we meld together. He presses his body into me again, and our rhythmic dance beneath the blankets continues – a dance we've fallen into almost by accident.

He breaks from the kiss, moving to my neck, his tongue exploring my skin, and I close my eyes again, focus on the sensation of Jeremiah on top of me and inside of me and all over me all at once.

Then his grip tightens around my waist, and he shudders, then relaxes. And I know it's over. At least for him.

I lick my lips. My heart pounds against the ribs of its cage, desperate to get out, and adrenaline still courses through my body. I am still primed, waiting for the moment he's clearly already had.

I bite back a sigh.

He strokes a strand of blonde hair out of my eyes and whispers, "you are so beautiful," like he stepped right out of a teenage rom-com, and I burst out laughing. I can't help it. All the magic of the moment—the sunshine, the smell, and the fact that my mom has been out of town for a week, thus giving me the perfect opportunity to lose my virginity—has flown right out the window, because now all I can think about is Jeremiah standing in front of the mirror practicing the exact perfect way to tell his girlfriend she's beautiful when she *finally* decides to have sex with him. It's too hilarious.

He scowls at me. "I'm trying to make this special, Dani." His body still presses against me from where he has me pinned under the covers, but he arches his back and props himself up on his elbows, leaning back so he can look me in the eye.

"I know. I'm sorry." I suck in my breath to stifle my next giggle. "But, c'mon. You sounded like you rehearsed that."

He shoves off of me, leaving me exposed on my bed, and shimmies back into his boxers. I sit up and snatch the blanket, pulling it up to my chest, though I guess what's the point? Not like I have anything to hide anymore. "Jer, c'mon. Don't be mad."

"I just wanted this to mean something. God, Dani, you can't take anything seriously, can you?"

"Yes, I can."

"Really?" he snorts. "Like when I asked you to Homecoming?" He folds his arms and glares at me. This is a sore subject between us.

"Well, it was really cheesy."

"It was meant to be a romantic gesture!"

I take a deep breath. "You sent a dozen roses to my homeroom." I push my hair behind my ears. "It was embarrassing. Everyone laughed at me."

"Who cares what other people think?"

"Everyone cares what other people think," I argue.

Well, most people do. Jeremiah… not so much. He's entirely sure of himself. He always has been. That's what attracted me to him in the first place. While I spent my hours at school hiding in the corners, he walked through the halls with his shoulders squared and his head held high. He's not even popular, not like the football players or the cheerleaders. He's simply self-assured. I watched him for weeks before finally working up the courage to pretend my pen was out of ink so I could ask to borrow his in our only shared class. Weeks. Not that Jeremiah could understand that, because he turned around, handed me the pen, then suggested I write my cellphone number in his notebook while I had it.

I about died. That kind of self-confidence needs to be bottled and sold in stores for people like me.

But that was almost a year ago. No more shyly worrying about what he thinks now. It's pretty obvious he's annoyed with me.

He sighs and leans his elbows on his legs, hiding his face in his hands.

Poor guy. I mean, he's only even wearing his boxers, and he just had sex for the first time, and his idiot girlfriend just had to ruin the moment.

That's me. Danielle Miller–moment killer.

It doesn't help that we've had this argument a million times already. Not necessarily always about Homecoming, but about how I don't care enough. I can't help it. Some people are born with the hyper-sensitive gene. They're just more in tune with the world, and nature, and the way everything is all connected. Like Jeremiah. He *feels* everything. And my Granny, a true hippie if ever there was one.

But not me. I try, honestly, I do. But then all my self-doubt comes creeping in, and I end up worrying more about getting through high school without making a complete fool of myself than about simply being myself. With Jeremiah, though, I can be myself.

I crawl across the bed and slide my arms around him, sneaking a kiss onto his neck, under his ear. He has a freckle there, one of my favorites. He's got a load of freckles, mostly on his shoulders and neck. I've got them practically memorized, courtesy of about a million make-out sessions this summer. All of which culminated in this, our not quite planned virginity-losing session.

That I had to ruin by laughing at the exact wrong time.

"You know I love you, right?" he mumbles.

"Of course," I kiss him again. "I love you, too. Even if I'm bad at showing it."

He lifts his head. "So, you don't regret… you know?" Oh God, so cute. He can't even say it.

"No!" I kiss him again. This time on the lips, tasting the layer of sweat accumulated there. "No way." I crawl onto his lap. "I love you, Jer. Times a gazillion. I'm happy."

"You sure?"

"Definitely." Of course I'm happy. I've been thinking about this moment just as long as he has. Maybe even longer. All summer, I've been debating back and forth. Do I do it? Do I not? How? When? What will I wear? Does it matter if I'm just going to take it off?

I've seriously never given anything this much thought before, but Jeremiah is worth it.

Then, just before she left town for the summer, my best friend, Shelby, made me swear not to overthink it. She knows how I can talk myself out of just about anything, if I'm nervous enough.

She wheeled me around the mall to help her pick out the perfect swimsuit for her vacation, offering skimpy suggestions of her own. "Wear this, and Jeremiah will fall over himself to get in your pants."

I pushed the bikini away. "I don't think he needs much encouragement."

"You can't make him wait forever," she said, giving me her know-it-all look. "Just relax and have fun."

Relax and have fun. Well, I did. It wasn't exactly how I pictured in my head, but I was with Jer, and I can't think of anything more perfect than that. For that, I'm happy. So very happy.

I run my fingers through his short brown hair, then kiss him again. "Are you mad at me?"

He wraps his arms around my waist. "No, I'm not mad at you." He squeezes me tighter, and I melt. I love when Jeremiah holds me around the waist, because he's really strong, even though he doesn't actually look it. That's what thirteen years of taekwondo will do for a guy. He can carry me up a flight of stairs without breaking a sweat, and he's done it before. Last February, when I twisted my ankle on the patch of ice at the movie theater, my hero lifted me up like nothing and carried me all the way back to the car.

His shoulders are to die for, all lean, rippling muscle. Shoulders that are already shifting beneath my arms as he sits up straighter. And that's not the only thing shifting.

He kisses me harder, and I gasp for breath as he rolls me over onto my back. His lips find their way to my collarbone, eliciting a light giggle. "Are we doing this again?" I whisper.

"If you want to." He pauses, mid-nibble, waiting for me to decide.

I grin. No regrets. "Yes!"

"You gonna laugh when I call you beautiful?"

"Yes!"

He growls, then climbs over me, and I can't help but laugh, this time a joyful peal that he soon joins with his own, deeper laughter.

For the record, I do *not* regret having sex with Jeremiah. I do, however, regret not making him use a condom.

Waxing Crescent

Dad's apartment drips tension. We're used to the late summer humidity, the way the warm air off the oceans permeates our town all summer long, even though we live an hour inland. But today, more than mere moisture fills the room. Today, my mom comes home from two weeks in Burundi distributing supplies and clean water.

Dad hides his nerves by flipping the TV to some baseball game, then opening up his laptop and pretending to work, so hidden that only his balding head is visible over the top of his computer. On the other hand, his long-time girlfriend, never a bride, Ashley, paces the floor and sucks hard on the cigarette which seems to be permanently lodged between her first two perfectly manicured fingers, then asks me, again, whether my mom's flight has landed yet.

I wave my phone. "She said she'd text. She hasn't texted."

Perky little Ashley has every reason to be nervous around my mom. She's been on Mom's blacklist since she started dating Dad, which was around three months before my parents officially separated, leading to the inevitable divorce. All this happened years ago, way before I was even aware of what cheating was, but I pieced it together in my own time.

Ever since Ashley and my dad moved in together, she's been downright terrified to be in the same room with Mom, which is hilarious and depressing at the same time. Even Dad's irritated with her, because he growls from behind his screen for her to sit down.

She does, but her leg still jiggles, shaking the whole sofa and making it difficult for me to relax. The smell of cigarette smoke doesn't help. For the life of me, I can't figure out how my dad is into that. If Jeremiah ever picked up smoking, I'd puke. Of course, he never would. He's very into health and wellness. He doesn't even drink caffeine.

My phone dings, and Ashley bolts to her feet.

"She just landed," I say dryly.

Dad closes his laptop. "Thirty minutes from the airport."

"Maybe I should stay in the bedroom while she's here," Ashley offers. I roll my eyes.

"Why?" Dad huffs. "This is your home too."

Dad has a way of taking his post-divorce anger out on anyone who dares to speak, and I'm not about to volunteer. I scroll through the apps on my phone for anything that could possibly amuse me for thirty minutes. Texting Jeremiah would be pointless. He's volunteering at some taekwondo summer camp for kids and has completely embraced the no technology rule there.

Ashley gets quiet and busies herself with some mundane task in the kitchen, and Dad shoots me a what-did-I-ever-do-to-deserve-this look, but if he's looking for sympathy from me, he's barking up the wrong tree, because he cheated on Mom with that idiot, and as Mom likes to say, "first you make your bed, then you sleep in it."

Of course, she's usually saying that to me and usually when I'm complaining about the consequences of some stupid mistake I've made, but I figure it applies to Dad as well.

I go back to my phone, finally landing on Instagram to amuse myself. Shelby has posted about a thousand pictures of her trip to Italy, and I can't help but feel a twinge of jealousy as I scroll through them. Shelby's family has money, and a lot of it. Enough to send her to Europe for the "cultural experience" every summer. When I asked Mom last year if she would consider letting me travel for "cultural experience," she suggested bringing me along to Burundi to help with the Earth's Bounty, the charity she works for. Shockingly enough, traipsing across Sub-Saharan Africa didn't really appeal to me, so I opted to stay home with Dad.

I wish I was with Shelby, exploring the Colosseum and riding scooters with sexy Italian boys. Maybe not that last part, Jeremiah might not like that.

My stomach has twisted into one gigantic jealous pretzel when the doorbell rings. Dad shuts his laptop slowly and climbs out of his easy chair. "Ready to go, Dani?"

I nod and head to the spare bedroom to get my things, but not before I hear Ashley's sing-song voice. "Ding dong, the witch is here."

I groan.

Dad's spare bedroom lacks personality of any kind. Where my bedroom at home is covered wall to wall with photographs of Jeremiah, Granny, Langley Beach, and everything important to me, this bedroom is beige, beige, and more beige. Beige curtains, beige walls, a plain brown and white quilted bedspread that Ashley clearly got at Bed, Bath, & Beyond. For a week, I've been sleeping in the most boring bedroom known to mankind, and I'm thrilled to finally be going home.

Jeremiah came and saved me from my beige hell-hole as often as he could but not often enough.

I set my tote bag on the bed and look around the room for anything I might have accidentally left behind. I can hear Mom's voice from the front door. It sounds stilted, like she's speaking through a forced smile. "Hello, Bert. Ashley. How was Dani's stay?"

"Good," Dad replies, with more force than necessary.

"Did you do anything fun while I was gone?"

I snort. Fun? At Dad's place? Ha. I already know how he's going to answer, though.

"We went bowling on Friday night."

Yup, bowling. That's Dad's idea of a fun family outing. He thinks I'm still seven years old, not sixteen.

I grab my bag and head to the bathroom to get my toothbrush, catching Mom's eye as I dart across the hall. She looks tan and healthy, her bright green eyes pop against her deepened skin tone. She offers me a smile as soon as she sees me.

"Anything else?" she asks Dad.

Dad sighs. "Well, she hung out with her boyfriend all day Saturday."

I freeze, my hand on the bathroom doorknob, and glance toward where

Mom is standing.

"I see," she says, her voice suddenly cold. She turns to look at me. "Doing what?"

"How should I know?" Dad asks. "They were out of the apartment."

Shit.

"Dani!" she calls, turning away from Dad. She's clearly decided he's useless.

"I have to get my stuff out of the bathroom."

"Come talk to me first. I haven't seen you in two weeks!" That syrupy sweet voice isn't going to fool me. I know I'm in for a lecture. I'm not a toddler anymore. I can't get fooled into coming to Mommy for a punishment just because she's pretending to be nice.

"Let me get my stuff first."

She drops the act. "Fine, but then we talk."

And just like that, I'm wishing she was back in Africa for another week or that I had told Dad to keep his fat mouth shut about Jeremiah. Why shouldn't I be allowed to spend time with my boyfriend? What's the worst that could happen?

I take my time packing up my makeup bag, even though I'm fairly easy going on the makeup. Some light foundation, eyeliner, and lip gloss. I never understand why some girls slather it on, I prefer the au natural look. I run my hairbrush through my hair a few times before packing it away. Any excuse to prolong the inevitable. I can hear her muffled voice through the doorway. "This was an opportunity for you to spend time with your daughter, Bert."

"I spent time with her."

"Sounds like she spent more time with her boyfriend," she retorts.

"Hey," he says, "what am I supposed to do? Lock her up and force her to hang out with me? She likes her boyfriend more. She's a teenager!"

Mom huffs. "And you're supposed to be a parent. You can say no, right? It's in your vocabulary? Or is everything just yes, yes, yes with you?"

"Jesus Christ, Hannah. Do you have to be so judgmental?"

Mom's gearing up to strike back, but I don't let her. I step out of the bathroom before she can say anything. "Hey, Mom."

Her sneer at Dad drops immediately. She holds out her arms to me for a hug, and I oblige, because even though I know she's mad that I snuck off to be with Jeremiah, she's still my mom, and I did miss her.

She squeezes me tight and plants a kiss on the top of my head. "I missed you Dani Pie."

"Oh my god, Mom. Don't call me that."

"Why?"

"It's embarrassing!"

She kisses me again, then lets me go. "You got all your things?"

"Yeah."

She nods, shoots Dad one last stern look, and walks out the door into the apartment's hallway. I wave bye to Dad, then follow her.

Waxing Gibbous

Mom has been home for six days, which is apparently all the time she needs to transition from Mother Theresa feeding the impoverished African children into overly-critical school shopping control freak. That she held on this long is really some sort of a miracle for her. Most years she's ready to buy out Target on the stroke of midnight, August first, like a shopaholic Cinderella. If she doesn't buy every planner in the store, she might turn back into a normal human being.

By the time I get downstairs, she's already making plans over breakfast, listing out stores to hit, what I need, the usual.

I lean across the table and peer at the list. "I can use the same backpack as last year, Mom."

She doesn't even look up. "Don't talk with your mouth full, Danielle." How did she even know?

I swallow the monster-sized bite of homemade French toast. Yeah, that's right. Homemade. My mom makes breakfast. She's really domestic. Mrs. Cleaver has nothing on my mom. "Sorry. But seriously, we don't need all this stuff."

"The styles may have changed. Don't you want to keep up with the latest fashions?"

Backpack fashion? Is that even a thing? "I'm pretty sure black canvas never goes out of style."

She purses her lips. "Fine," she says as she scratches *backpack* off the long list. "But you still need new clothes, and notebooks and…"

She keeps going, but I'm already in my own world. New clothes aren't such a bad idea. I've been living in jeans and plain colored T-shirts for years, but Jeremiah made a comment last spring about how pretty I look in a skirt, and now I'm dreaming of something short and tight that would make him go absolutely wild.

"Dani?" Mom's voice makes me jump. "Are you listening?"

"No."

She sighs. "I was saying, I thought maybe you'd like to drive. You can put in some more practice to get your license."

I scowl. This is her underhanded way of reminding me that I have failed spectacularly because I didn't get my license when I turned sixteen last April. She finds a way to sneak her never-ending disappointment of me into practically every conversation.

"No thanks," I mutter.

"I thought maybe you could try the test again before school starts."

Oh brother. She's not going to drop it. I shrug and stand up, leaving my dirty plate behind. "I can ride with Jeremiah everywhere."

"But he's going to college next fall. What will you do then?"

See, this is the problem with my mom. She focuses on obstacles over a year away. Who cares what's going to happen in a year?

"When Jeremiah leaves, then I'll get my license. No big deal."

Mom eyes my plate. She's itching to nag me about leaving my dirty dishes around. I know she is. But it's hard, because she can't interrupt the get-your-license nag in favor of the clean-up-after-yourself nag. She has to pick and choose. Just as she's about to burst, I grab my dish and walk it to the sink, saving her the trouble.

She breathes a sigh of relief. "Don't you want to be like the rest of your friends?"

Cue my massive eyeroll.

First of all. No. No way. Never. The last thing I want to be is like every other brain-dead teenager at my school.

Second, they are not my friends. You know how in preschool your teacher refers to every single kid in the class as your "friend?" That's my mom. I could see the most douchiest of douchebags at the mall, and my mom would say, "Oh Dani, introduce me to your friend!"

Not my friends. No way.

I only have two friends. Jeremiah, who is really my boyfriend, and I love him to pieces. And Shelby, who I've known since eighth grade when she stood up in our science class and asked Mrs. Kenzie how to spell "scrotum" during our reproductive system unit. When Mrs. Kenzie answered, Shelby jutted out her hip, raised her eyebrow in the absolute coolest way ever, and said, "Wow! You're really on *the ball*, Mrs. K!"

The whole class laughed, and she's been my best friend ever since. Anyone who can torture uptight bitches like Mrs. Kenzie like that is cool in my book.

I guess, technically, Shelby's boyfriend, Miles, is kind of my friend, but he doesn't really talk so much as grunt, so it's kind of hard to tell.

Mom's not done nagging, though. "I just don't think you applied yourself."

Yup. She's got me there. *Not applying myself* has become my go-to mode over the years. All part of my master plan to drive her crazy. At least that's what she thinks. Really, I just don't want to be noticed. I've watched enough teen rom-coms to know that every school has the same types of people. The over-eager kids who raise their hands at every single question. The assholes who just try to cause problems. The jocks who everyone is supposed to fawn over 24/7. The purposefully "fringe" elements.

Then there are people like me.

The invisibles.

I love being invisible. Anything I can do to skate through the four years of hell at James Polk High so I can get as far away as possible. Just me and Jer, and the ocean. He's promised me the ocean.

It drives Mom insane, because as much as I *don't apply,* she is right there, over-applying.

Think the perfect mom—head of the PTA, in the Booster Club. Hell, she even ran for a seat on the home owner's association, so now she officially has the authority to chew out neighbors who dare to show up at the pool when they haven't paid their dues. I've seen her do it.

On paper, she's like Super Mom. Home cooked meals three times a day, all perfectly balanced and nutritious. She packs my lunch for school, like every day, and writes a personalized note. So embarrassing. She attends every single event our school hosts, helps organize all the fundraisers, donates homemade brownies to every bake sale, and to top it all off, she looks great too! Always in fashion, always perfectly made up, hair in a stylish bob. I can't compete with that.

Long story short, I do everything in my power not to join anything. Mom's already joined enough for both of us.

"I just didn't see the point." I argue as I rinse my plate. "Like I said, Jer will drive me around."

She opens her mouth to continue, but I'm done. I escape up the stairs, taking them two at a time. I can't stay hidden in my bedroom for long, because within ten minutes, she knocks on my door to remind me to get dressed to go shopping.

Jeans, blue T-shirt, and black sneakers. Done.

* * *

I spend the entire car ride texting Shelby. She's been out of town all summer, and she just got back last night. It's been a long summer without Shelby to talk to. Jeremiah's great, but he's not interested in "girl talk" as he calls it. I've been dying to tell Shelby about Jeremiah and me for the past week. She spent all spring encouraging me to "take the plunge" with Jer, because, as she puts it, "guys like Jeremiah won't wait forever."

Except Jeremiah is perfect, and I know he'd wait a million years for me. That's how much he loves me. He even said so.

I didn't make him wait though, because I love him too, and it felt so right, and he really is amazing.

I send Shelby about a dozen texts, trying to play it cool. Mostly stuff like, "I wanna hear about Europe" or "let's catch up," because I don't want to seem clingy. She never answers, so I stuff the phone back in my bag.

"I really wish you wouldn't spend all day looking at a screen," Mom says as she turns into the mall's parking lot.

Here we go. Yet another diatribe about screen time and the teen's brain development. My mom, being Super Mom, has read practically every article ever written about raising a child in the Digital Age. She even wrote a few and published them on her blog. How does she even find the time? I don't get it. Not that it matters. It only takes one person at our school finding that blog, and my affected invisibility will be long gone.

"I do not spend all day on my phone."

"Really?" she scoffs. She puts the car in park and looks at me. "So, what did you do all summer?"

Busted. A whole lotta Netflix. "Nothing."

"That's my point, Dani." She unbuckles her seat belt and climbs out of the car, assuming, correctly, that I will follow. "Other kids your age have jobs or they volunteer. Or both! Those sorts of things look good on a college application. Doesn't that matter to you?"

I shrug. Not really.

"You're not going to have Jeremiah to hang onto all your life." Then she completes the statement with a raised eyebrow and pursed lips. The only thing she's missing is the disapproving shake of the head.

Shows what she knows. Jer and I are lasting forever. Not that I can tell her that. Not without getting the "Dad" lecture.

The "Dad" lecture is her favorite. Dad and her got hitched right out of high school. She hadn't even had another boyfriend. Still hasn't, not that I can tell. Then, Dad started banging the 22-year-old he met at work. Now they have their stupid little apartment on the other side of town, and I get guilted into going bowling with him every other Friday night. It's pathetic, and even though she would never admit it, Mom's still pretty angry about the whole thing. Who wouldn't be?

So, instead of defending Jeremiah, who would *never* cheat on me, I just shrug again.

That really fires her up. "You should be interacting with real people, Dani! Making real friends. Remember freshman year when you joined the bowling league?"

Do I ever. What a waste of time. Nothing says "loser with a capital L" like being on the school's bowling league. Shelby kept making fun of me, so I quit. I wasn't any good anyway. I only joined because Dad wanted me to. I guess I thought it would give us something in common. But after he and Ashley moved in with each other, I just didn't care anymore.

"You need real friends," Mom says.

"I have real friends. Shelby's my friend."

Mom looks like she wants to say something, but she holds back. She's not a huge fan of Shelby, because Shelby doesn't put up with her Perfect Mom shtick. Mom grabs the handle on the mall's front door and yanks it open. "Let's just get this over with." It's her favorite time of the year, and she's already sick of spending it with me.

Moment successfully ruined.

"Yeah," I mumble. I guess shopping with your daughter is just something one has to *get over with* these days.

Waxing Gibbous

For some weird reason, our school insists on starting on a Thursday every year. I don't get it. Two extra days of summer vacation completely wasted. Why not just wait until the next Monday? No one has ever taken the first two days seriously.

Except my mom, of course. She wakes up thirty minutes early on the first day of school, for the specific purpose of "making sure I look my best." Jeans and T-shirts are strictly forbidden. I anticipate her disapproval and opt straight for the blue and green plaid mini-skirt we bought the week earlier.

She eyes my legs as I walk into the kitchen, but ultimately decides not to say anything. Sure, it's a little short, but if she didn't want me wearing it, she shouldn't have bought it, right?

"Do you want me to drive you to school?" she asks as she slides two sunny-side up eggs onto a plate and sets it on the kitchen island where I usually eat breakfast.

I shake my head. "Jer's picking me up." I check the time on my phone with my free hand as I spoon eggs and hash browns into my mouth with the other. I'm so busy, I don't even notice my mom walk around to the back of my chair until she starts messing with my hair.

"Geez, Mom! What are you doing?"

"You had a few fly-aways. I was just smoothing them for you."

I bat her hand away. "Well, don't. God, I can take care of myself."

She raises her hands defensively. "Okay, okay. I'm sorry." But she doesn't look sorry. She slides onto her stool and taps her fingers on the counter. She gets all jittery every school year, like it's some big deal or something.

"I just want you to look your best. When you look your best, you feel your best." How many times have I heard that before? Too many.

I roll my eyes. "Thanks for telling me I don't look good."

"Oh, honey, of course you do."

"But not as good as you want me to." We've been through this song and dance before.

Mom sniffs. "Why does everything have to be an argument with you?"

Thank God Jer texts me at that precise moment and saves me from having to answer *that* question. What a question. Maybe because she's so overbearing, I never feel like I can just breathe and be myself. But try telling her that. I guarantee, the second I say to her that she needs to lighten up, she will break her back trying to prove that she *has* lightened up. It's an endless cycle. I've given up fighting it.

I stand up. "Jer's here."

"Is he going to come in?"

"Doubt it." I grab my bag off the floor and dart to the door. "See ya."

She follows a step behind me. "Have a good first day."

"Whatever." Good first day. Ha. This is high school after all.

Jer has already climbed out of his car and walked halfway up the sidewalk when I burst through the front door. I guess maybe he was going to come inside. What a gentleman. All the better, because as soon as I see him, I launch into his arms.

"Wow," he says as he lifts me up. "You look amazing."

See, Mom? Was that so hard? For her, it is. She doesn't even know how to turn off the gotta-find-fault-in-everything-Dani-does part of her brain. I'm pretty sure when I was a kid, she walked around behind me correcting me when I played with my toys wrong.

"Thanks," I whisper, then I plant a kiss on his lips. Lip gloss be damned. I can always fix it in the car.

He responds immediately, pulling me tighter, and after another long kiss, wrenches his lips away. "We have to go to school, Dani."

"Do we really?" I tease.

He raises an eyebrow. "Yes." Jer's a rule follower, one-hundred percent.

Skipping school is a completely foreign concept to him. Not that I would skip either, but mostly because I imagine my mom would have an ulcer or something if she found out. For Jer, it's all about getting into a good college, so he can provide for a family someday. The honorable man thing has been drilled into him for years now, which I love. Because a guy like Jer—who always does the right thing—is pretty hard to come by these days.

I pull away, sliding my hands down his shoulders to his chest. "Lucky you. You get to leave next year."

"And you'll be right behind me."

"Definitely." I give him one last kiss. "Okay, let's go." I cast one last glance back at the house and see my mom standing in the doorway watching us, with hands on her hips and a magazine-ready smile plastered on her face. As soon as she catches my eye, she waves.

I can't get one moment of peace around that woman. Ugh.

As soon as Jer pulls into the street, I yank my hair out of its ponytail and give it a good ruffle. "Have you talked to Shelby lately?"

Jer shakes his head no.

I cast one last glance back at my house, where Mom is still watching. "She's been back for over a week and she hasn't texted me once." It's really weird. Shelby is more addicted to her social media than I am. She practically lives for her followers, racking them up by the hundreds. A real trend-setter. But she's been silent all summer.

"I'm sure she'll be at school, and she'll tell you all about her amazing summer in France."

"Italy," I remind him.

"Sorry. Italy." He says it with a bit of an attitude. Jer has a chip on his shoulder about Shelby and her money, because his family is strictly working class. His dad is a welder for some factory the next town over, and Shelby's been known to be a bit condescending when it suits her. I guess if you have the kind of rep that she does, you can get away with it.

I grab his hand and squeeze. "Four years of college, then law school, and you'll be making the big bucks. Then you can go to France or Italy or wherever you want." With a coy smile, I bring his hand to my lips and plant a kiss. "Just remember to bring me along."

His shoulders relax and he grins. "Yeah. Someday."

* * *

Since Jeremiah's a senior, he has homeroom with the other seniors. Senior homeroom—so I've heard—is basically forty-five minutes of goofing around and planning the winter ski trip. What they do after winter break, I have no idea. I've never been friends with a senior before.

Junior homeroom, on the other hand, is all about bettering yourself as a person, and making plans for the future. Boring. They push the college agenda, of course, because apparently everyone needs to go to college these days. I'm anticipating forty-five minutes of my mom's usual lectures in someone else's voice.

The only good thing about it is that Shelby and I are in the same class. Sure enough, I walk in, and there she is, smacking her gum and leaning back in her chair so far that I'm sure she'll fall over any second. Shelby is my exact opposite in every way. Instead of long blonde hair like me, she's got these dark brown curls that she keeps cut close to her head. She's outgoing and flirtatious, definitely not like me. She actually likes to be the center of attention. She wouldn't seem like the sort of person I'd want to hang out with, but she's actually the perfect cover. When I'm around Shelby, all eyes are on her. She's positively magnetic. I go completely unnoticed. Just how I like it.

Sure enough, she doesn't even see me walk into the room, she's too busy flirting with the guy sitting behind her.

I slide into the seat next to her. "Hey."

She glances over. "Oh, hey Dani."

Other people might have freaked out that she was being so dismissive, but not me. I get it. For Shelby, flirting is an art form. She can't break stride once she starts. Eventually, the bell rings, and in walks—I glance at my schedule—Mr. Craig.

"Good morning, juniors," he says with his arms spread wide. "Welcome,

welcome. Welcome to your penultimate year of public education." He settles onto the stool at the front of the room and waits until every eye turns to him. "Welcome to our year. This year," he pauses, "we will be accessing our souls."

I glance at Shelby, and she has a look on her face that borders between pure glee and utter shock. I know she can't wait to tear this guy down. I turn back to Mr. Craig. He's waiting for someone to ask what he means. But not me. I don't volunteer anything in class, ever. Everyone is silent, and the seconds tick by as each of us waits for someone else to raise their hand.

"Our souls," he says, and he stands. He thumps his fist against his chest. "Our souls. Our very essence of being. What makes us human? What makes us alive? What makes our hearts beat in our chests? What makes our everyday have meaning? Why do we continue to climb out of those beds of ours each morning, ready to face the day? What do we hope to accomplish? What makes you… you?" He looks down at his roster. "Danielle Miller!"

Oh God, why me? Talk about my worst nightmare.

Every face in the room turns to me. I am the sun, and they are the sunflowers, their faces follow me. If only I could find a nice cloud to duck behind.

"Danielle? Come on up!" The level of enthusiasm he's displaying should be banned during the first week of school.

Shelby stifles laughter behind her fist as I climb out of my seat.

"Come on." Mr. Craig gestures for me to hurry. "Don't be shy."

I trudge up to the front of the room, suddenly aware that all the skin on my legs is exposed for my classmates. Not jeans. Not a T-shirt. Just a whole lotta leg. My cheeks burn.

When I reach the front of the room, Mr. Craig spins me around by my shoulders to face the class. "Danielle. Tell us. Why are you here?"

"Uh… because I have to be?"

"You have to be?" He has this booming, overly enthusiastic voice. I wonder whether it'll last the whole year. Most teachers start to sound tired and cranky by November. But something tells me Mr. Craig may last until spring.

"I mean, aren't we required to go to school?" I ask.

Mr. Craig cocks his head. "At sixteen? You could drop out."

I grin. What an idea. "My mom would kill me."

Shelby blurts out. "What kind of teacher are you? Encouraging your students to drop out?"

Other teachers would have punished her for the interruption. But Mr. Craig doesn't even look up. "I didn't mean why are you at school. I meant, why are you here? On this Earth? Why do you exist?"

The class goes silent. Definitely my worst nightmare. The obvious answer is that about seventeen years ago, my parents had sex, but I'm pretty sure he doesn't want to hear about that. I opt for the tried and true, "I don't know." Most teachers will let that slide and move onto another victim.

"Well," Mr. Craig's hand lands on my shoulder. "That is what I hope we find out by the end of the year." He nudges me back to my seat, then turns to address the class. "A purpose, ladies and gentleman. That is what we need. Now. In this year. Before you apply for colleges, before you make plans for after you leave school, before you do any of that awful 'adult' stuff. Now. Here. Find your purpose. Find your *raison d'être*. Access your soul."

"What do you love?"

Jeremiah.

"What do you care about?"

Jeremiah.

"What makes you want to continue living on this heartless rock day after day?"

Geez, this is getting dark.

"But first, introductions!"

We spend the rest of homeroom filling out those typical "get to know you" worksheets that teachers bombard us with at the beginning of every year. Favorite color, favorite TV show, blah blah blah. Except, when we hand them in to Mr. Craig at the end of the hour, he glances down at the stack, cries "this isn't really you!" and tosses them into the recycling bin.

What a waste.

* * *

Jeremiah laughs when we tell him at lunch. "Oh yeah, I should have told you about Mr. Craig. He's a bit out there." He loops his arm around my waist while he eats, pulling me close. His fingers play with the waistband of my skirt, and it makes me smile.

"I think he's interesting," I reply.

"I think he's a weirdo," Shelby says as she sits across from me and pulls a Tupperware container out of her bag. "Total freak and probably a pervert too."

Jeremiah raises an eyebrow.

"You think everyone's a pervert," I argue.

"Everyone usually is." Shelby starts eating, but as soon as Miles sits next to her, she abandons her food in favor of him. She's a very physical person, and I know for a fact she's been written up for PDA, aka making out in the hallway, more than anyone else at our school. Sure enough, her fingers are curling into Miles's hair within seconds, and she leans over and starts to nibble on his neck.

"Some of us are trying to eat," Jeremiah says pointedly.

"Some of us are sounding jealous," Shelby shoots back.

Jer throws his food down and stands up. "I'm outta here."

"Wait, Jer, she was just joking," I say, but he just shakes his head.

"I have to get to class." He grabs his tray and walks it back to the trash. My eyes follow him as he returns the tray then trudges out the door. Then he's gone.

I glare across the table. "Thanks a lot."

"It's not my fault he's so uptight." She goes back to Miles.

I shove my half-eaten sandwich back into my lunch box. "I'm going to head to class, too."

* * *

I catch up with Jeremiah at his locker after school. "Hey, sorry about lunch."

He shrugs. "Just Shelby being Shelby. Why are you sorry?"

Because she's my friend. But it feels weird to say that out loud. "I dunno." I watch as Jer carefully stacks his textbooks in his locker, making sure they're in order for his classes tomorrow, before shutting the door and spinning the lock. When he's done, I slide my hand into his, lacing my fingers through his. "Want to come to over? My mom's still at work, so we could… um…" I bite my lip at gaze up at him through my eyelashes, putting on what I hope is the perfectly flirty girlfriend look.

At first, I think it works. He leans down and kisses my cheek, letting his jaw rest against my cheek longer than strictly necessary. His free hand curls around my waist, and a flutter of desire runs through my body.

Then he pulls away. "I can't today, Dani. Sorry. Taekwondo."

Oh yeah, I had forgotten. On Thursdays, he helps with the beginner kid classes.

"No problem." My voice comes out higher pitched than normal.

"Tomorrow—" he begins.

"I'll be at my dad's," I say, "Friday night bowling."

His shoulders slump. "Oh."

This isn't how this is supposed to go. Every time I imagined sleeping with Jer, I imagined a deeper connection between us. A whole new world of exciting adventures we could have together. But now, it seems like things keep getting in the way.

Maybe this kind of setback would break up other couples, but Jer and I are stronger than this. I trace his jaw with my fingers, then slide my hand around the back of his neck, then kiss him hard. "Maybe I'll come by your house after," I whisper into his lips.

I feel his mouth curl into a smile beneath mine. "Sounds good."

Full Moon

I trudge down the stairs Saturday morning and am immediately greeted with The Look. Mom gets it every time she wants to talk about the future. I've only been back in school two days, but already she wants to start. The big talk. She wanted to do it last night, but it was bowling night with my dad, so she couldn't. She has this stupid philosophy that bowling nights are *his* nights, and she doesn't want to encroach on his time. I think she assumes that if given half the chance, I'd rather spend the time alone in my bedroom ignoring her than at the town's tiny lane with Dad.

And she'd be right.

Dad and I finished our bowling session around nine, still early enough for me to hang with Jer for a couple hours, so I convinced him to drop me off. His parents were home, so we couldn't really do anything except watch a movie in his room and make out, but that's better than nothing. By the time Jer drove me home, Mom was already asleep, so I just snuck up to my room.

But now she's watching me with narrowed eyes, and I know she wants to talk. I have to come up with a good reason to get the hell out of the house or else she'll be nagging me all day about big goal stuff. Have I started looking at colleges? Have I thought about what I want to do after I leave school?

The short answer is, I'm going wherever Jeremiah is going, and I just want to write. I have Mr. Craig for Creative Writing as well as homeroom, and even though he's spent the last two days engaging us in discussions about the "purpose of artistic expression," I'm thrilled to have an opportunity to write about what I want instead of boring essays.

When Mom opens her mouth to ask me what I'm doing today, I already have my answer prepared.

"Going to see Granny," I say before she can get a word out.

She can't argue with that, because visiting Granny is practically community service. Granny's been in a nursing home for about four years now—ever since she started showing signs of Alzheimer's. She's been deteriorating fast. I'm not even sure she knows who I am anymore, but I try to visit her at least once a month.

Mom visits her every Monday. Once a week, like clockwork, she spends exactly one hour with her mother. I don't even know what they talk about, or if they do. I do know that Mom takes her knitting with her, and she gets vastly more of it done in her hour with Granny than she ever does with her knitting club. I don't think she and Granny talk much.

"Do you want me to come along?" she asks.

"Not really."

Mom sighs. "I can drive you."

I grimace and start for the door. "I'll just ride my bike."

"Don't be silly. It'll take you forever."

"No, it won't."

"You wouldn't have this problem if you had your license." Mom follows me out the door. The driver's license argument again. When will she ever be done with it?

I unlock my bike and pull it away from the railing. "Stop bugging me about it, Mom! I'll get my license when I get it." I don't want to hear her response, so I swing my leg over my bike and start peddling.

Sure, it takes about forty-five minutes to get to the nursing home, but it's a nice day. We're close enough to the ocean, I can smell the salt in the air, especially on warm days like today, but far enough away that it's not unbearably humid. I relax and breathe the fresh air, and forget all about Mom and her plans. When I get there, I leave my bike in the rack and walk inside.

"Hey, Minnie."

The nurse at the front desk looks up. "Oh, hello, Danielle. Here to see your gran?"

I lean on the counter in front of her. "Yeah, how is she?"

She slides a clipboard toward me to sign. "Well you know. Good days and bad days."

"And today?"

"A good day."

I smile. "Good." I sign my name on the guest list and hand the clipboard back. "Where is she?"

"In her room."

Good. I know it sounds horrible, but honestly, I just can't handle being around all the old people sometimes. Granny is one thing. But everyone else? They always want to talk to me. It's like they've never seen a teenager before. All those questions.

"Where do you go to school?"

"What's your favorite subject?"

"How are your friends?"

"What do you want to do when you graduate?"

None of their business, if you ask me.

When Mom suggested I start volunteering there to pad my college applications, I thought I was going to die. She hasn't mentioned it since.

This morning, I slide past the rec room and make my way down the familiar hallway to stop in front of my gran's room, knocking as I push the door open. "Granny?"

She's awake and sitting in her armchair. That's a good sign. She's not feeling too sick to get out of bed. And she looks genuinely happy to see me. "Oh, hi! Come in, come in!"

Maybe I'm biased, but my Granny's not like all the other old ladies in this place. For one, she still has long thick hair, gray now, instead of blonde, but still wavy like mine. I spent my entire childhood braiding that hair before trips to the ocean and seeing it hang loose over her shoulder now has my fingers itching to gather, separate, and twist again.

"I hope you don't mind me stopping by." But I'm already in. Granny's always been my go-to person, especially whenever Mom was completely impossible to talk to. She gets me. Or, she used to.

"No, of course not, dear."

I pad across the room, lean over Granny to give her a strong hug, then pull the guest chair—an uncomfortable hard plastic contraption that I swear was designed to discourage visitors—closer to her. "How are you feeling?"

"Oh good. That storm last night, though, kept me up. I told Harold to close the blinds, but he couldn't be bothered."

There wasn't a storm last night, and Harold, my Granddad, has been dead for two years. But I know better than to argue. "I'm sorry, Granny."

"Oh, it's quite all right, Hannah. Quite all right."

Hannah. Oh God. That's my mom's name. Granny's never called me by my mom's name before. I suppose we look alike, blonde hair and all, but still.

"Granny, I'm not Hannah. I'm her daughter. Danielle?"

Granny squints her eyes at me. "What? Oh… yes… Danielle?"

"Yeah."

She doesn't look so sure. Her eyes dart around the room. "But that storm last night. That storm. I hope it didn't bother the baby?"

She's completely gone, so I just play along. I read somewhere that's what you're supposed to do with Alzheimer's patients. Go along with what they're saying. "No, Granny. The baby was fine."

"Poor boy," she mutters. "And poor you. But don't you worry, Hannah. He'll sleep through the night, eventually. They all do. They all do."

I don't answer. I can't really. She's talking about Caleb, my older brother. Or he was my older brother, except he died when I was still a baby. He was only four or five, I'm not even sure. It's hard to tell from the pictures, and Mom never talks about him. Strictly forbidden.

We sit in silence for a while, then Granny blinks bright blue eyes at me. "What were we talking about?"

"Oh, uh…" I shrug. "School started up again."

"Oh, yes, Dani. How is school?"

Good, she knows it's me again. "Good, I guess. I mean, we've only had two days."

She smiles and nods. But her eyes are already glazing over again. She's thinking about something else. "Don't you worry about the baby, Hannah."

And she's back on that. Not a good day. I don't know what Minnie was talking about. I excuse myself, standing up to leave. "Granny, I gotta go."

"Go? So soon?"

"Yeah, well, I told Jeremiah I'd meet him." Not true, but she'll never know the difference.

She nods. "Very well. Very well. I'll see you tomorrow?"

"Um. Maybe."

"Yes, good. And Hannah?"

I wince. "Yeah?"

"Don't you worry about that boy of yours. He's going to be just fine. Just fine."

Or not.

I lean over and hug her. "Thanks, Granny."

I take my time biking home, and by the time I get up that last hill, my calves are killing me. Maybe I should get my license. I bet I could convince Jeremiah to let me take the test in his car. I just can't learn with my mom. She spends the whole time second-guessing everything I do, and then I get nervous and start making mistakes, which just makes her freak out and try to control everything.

When I get home, Mom is sitting at the dining room table, working on her mailing list for the home owner's association when I walk in the front door. She looks up for half a second, then goes back to folding paper and licking envelopes. "How was your grandmother?"

"Not a good day," I mutter.

"Oh?"

I walk over to the table and drop into the chair farthest from her. "She thought I was you."

She doesn't look up. "I'm sorry. That must have been hard for you."

I can't tell how she means that, so I just try to ignore it. "I'm going to head to my room, if that's okay?"

Mom lets out an enormous sigh.

"Or... not?"

She starts rifling around in all her papers. "I could really use your help around here, Dani. I can't do everything myself, you know." Which is a surprise, because it seems like she survives on a mixture of doing-everything-herself and nagging-her-daughter-to-death with a dash of always-maintain-appearances for flavor.

It's not so much that she has to be a part of everything, but she just acts like it's such an imposition on her. Like she's not the one piling a thousand responsibilities on herself, then complaining when she has to do everything.

She never learned to delegate. But that's on her. Not my problem.

I sink back into my chair. "What are you doing?"

"HOA business." She doesn't elaborate.

"You can't tell me?" I ask. "It's top secret stuff?"

She sighs and puts the paper in her hands down. "I'm sorry, Dani. I didn't think you cared about HOA business."

Now I can definitely hear the sarcasm, but she just keeps going. "If you must know, we're having a meeting in two weeks to swear in new board members and discuss installing a locking gate on the pool. I am mailing out ballots to everyone in the neighborhood to gauge interest and remind them to come to the meeting. I am also sending special reminders to board members about the HOA requirements regarding community cleanup and—"

"Okay, okay. Sorry I asked. What do you want me to do?"

She shoves a pile of envelopes my way. "Stuff and lick."

I groan and pick up the top envelope. Nothing I can do to get out of it now. Luckily, the stress from HOA seems to have made her forget all about the Big Talk she was dying to have this morning. Another conversation successfully averted. I can't help but smile to myself as I fold pamphlets into thirds and slide them into envelopes.

As soon as I finish, I stand up. If I don't get away now, I'll get roped into another mindless chore. Too late, as my foot hits the first step of the stairs, she calls after me.

"Dani, you need to start a load of laundry. And make sure you separate the whites!"

As if she would ever let me forget.

Waning Gibbous

The sea is my mother
Grand and warm.
Demanding and harsh
Unyielding
Its waves are her arms
They embrace me, buoy me, then send me reeling
Head over heels
Drowning in expectations

* * *

A week and a half into the school year, and things are starting to settle in. I'm back to being invisible, at least to most of my teachers. Mr. Craig clearly doesn't believe in invisible teenagers, because he makes sure to call on me at least once every single day, in both classes. Always with these big deep questions about the meaning of life. And there I am, answering the same way every time.

"I don't know."

I keep hoping, eventually he'll realize that I'll never know, and he'll move on. But I'm not holding my breath. He seems like the sort of teacher who expects everyone to figure out the meaning of life, eventually. I can't tell whether he's a genius or whether he's insane.

I'm pulling books out of my locker on Thursday between classes when Shelby swings by, with way more energy than anyone should be allowed to have. Maybe I'm just dragging. I have been feeling tired lately.

She loops an arm around my shoulder. "What are you doing tomorrow night?"

"I dunno," I say. "Probably just going over to Jeremiah's house."

"Don't."

I raise an eyebrow. "Why not?"

She grins. "No, I mean, we're going out, all of us. Miles's older brother is back for Labor Day weekend, and they're doing this big bonfire. We're all going. You and Jeremiah, Miles and me. Bunch of college boys." She gets this gleam in her eye.

"Um…" This sounds like Shelby's sort of thing, the big crowd, the flirting with strange boys, but not mine.

She won't take no for an answer. "Wear something sexy!" And she's off before I can respond. I make my way to Jeremiah's locker. He's got one of the nice lockers in the senior hallway, of course. He closes it just as I walk up.

"Hey," he says, grinning as he slides his hand in mine and leans down to kiss me. "I was just coming to get you. Apparently, Shelby and Miles are doing this thing…"

"Yeah," I interrupt him. "Shelby just told me. You wanna go?"

He shrugs. "Could be fun."

I raise an eyebrow. "Really?"

"It'll get us out of town for the night. Away from the parents…" He lets that last part linger between us. I know exactly what he's thinking.

I swear, my Mom has some extra-sensory detector, because the second Jeremiah and I start making out at my house, she's knocking on my door or barging into the living room. Basically, we haven't had sex in weeks now. And we can't at his house, because he has about a thousand brothers and sisters. There's never any privacy.

Honestly, a night away sounds perfect. "Alright, let's do it."

So that Friday when school lets out, instead of our usual meandering around town in Jeremiah's car, the two of us head out east toward the ocean. I can already smell the salt in the air.

"Where is this thing?" I ask.

Jeremiah turns onto the highway. "Didn't Shelby tell you? It's at Langley Beach."

I smile. Langley Beach is where Granny used to take me every summer. I've made so many good memories there—wading in the salt water, searching for shells in the sand. Throwing rocks into the waves. Climbing to the top of the abandoned lighthouse.

"No, she didn't say."

It's an hour drive to get there. I know the way almost by heart, though I've never driven it myself, of course. One hour of perfection. I slide my hand into Jeremiah's as he drives, squeezing every few minutes, to remind him I'm still here. He squeezes back, and I can feel his anticipation through his skin. This isn't just a bonfire to blow off steam. This isn't just a trip to the beach.

This is us. Our chance to be alone.

The sun is low behind us by the time we pull into the parking spaces, and we can see the light of flames already dancing on the beach. Hoots rise up into the darkening sky, along with sparks of flame, the voices of wild college-aged boys and girls howling to the full moon. Jeremiah slides a hand around my waist as we walk up the wooden stairs and over the sandy dune.

And it's perfect.

Shelby and Miles are dancing along with the rest of the group, the firelight playing on her dark curls.

I turn to Jeremiah. "Do you want to join them?"

"Do you?" There's a half-smile forming at the corner of his mouth.

"No," I kiss him softly. "Let's just walk along the beach."

"You won't be too cold?"

I shake my head. "It's still summer." Even though it's starting to feel like fall. The air is turning. I can feel it. The wind comes off the ocean and plays in my long blonde hair. I wish, for a second, I had pulled it back. But no. Tonight, I am a child of the ocean and of the moon. Like Granny says. We are all children of the Earth and stars. Tonight, I will be one with the sea.

And with Jeremiah.

As we walk, I pull my sandals off my feet so I can feel the wet sand squish between my toes. We walk long enough for the sun to fully set, and the only lights come from the moon and the stars. The bonfire is far behind us, reduced to a distant orange glow and faint, musical laughter. The moon pulls the tide high, and the water splashes around my ankles. Jeremiah rolls his pants up to his knees.

His fingers lace in mine, and he rubs his thumb along the ridges of my hand while we stroll. The air is warm, but when the breeze rises off the ocean, I shiver and lean into him. The beach bends around some rocks, the lighthouse looms ahead of us. Finally, we're alone.

Truly alone.

We don't exchange words. We don't need to. We simply head straight for the lighthouse and climb the stairs to the platform at the top, just wide enough for the two of us. Jeremiah pulls his jacket off and lays it on the floor, and then we sit on top of it.

He slides his fingers through my hair. "Is this good?"

"Yes."

It is. So good. So very good. When he leans forward, and presses his lips to mine. So very good. I don't think about each moment. Each little thing. They're fluid. They run into each other, like a river into the ocean. The vast ocean.

Instead, I think about the waves, breaking on the stone below us. Like Jeremiah, they move with a steady rhythm. And I move with him. As the tide comes in, the waters grow angry, turbulent, dangerous. But in Jeremiah's arms, I am safe and loved.

The steady rise and fall over the water, and the steady rise and fall of Jeremiah's body. The water splashes on the beach below us, the high tide has come in. Soon it will retreat. But for now, we are one with the ocean. I nuzzle into Jeremiah's chest, breathing in the salty scent of him, and I watch his eyes. They shine with happiness. His chest rises and falls with the exertion, and I rise and fall with it. Then, with one long sigh, he looks at me and smiles.

I mouth the words we've said a thousand times. *I love you.* I don't want the crash of the waves to be ruined by our silly human emotions.

He understands, just like he understands everything about me. *I love you, too*, comes the silent reply.

We wait out the high tide. The water which danced around the base of the lighthouse now sinks back to the ocean, leaving only wet sand and scurrying creatures behind. It's time. We both know it. We have to go back. I stand first and smooth my skirt. I try to finger tangles out of my hair, but it's too far gone, knotted from our exertions. I'll brush it as we drive home.

As we step out of the building, Jeremiah checks his watch, its green glow a cruel reminder of man's interference in Mother Nature's domain. "It's late," he says. "I doubt we'll get home before eleven."

That sends a chill down my spine. "Mom's not gonna like that."

Jeremiah gives a sheepish shrug. "Want me to talk to her?"

"No," I say with a shake of my head. "I better call her on the drive home though."

We trudge back to his car, our fingers laced. Even though I know I should be worried about what my mom says. Even though I know I stayed out way past curfew without her permission.

I don't care.

Because, I finally feel like I'm where I should be, with the right person.

* * *

"Hold it," Jeremiah throws a strong arm in front of me, stopping my progress down the beach.

"What?"

He points to the ground. "The crabs are coming out."

Sure enough, the tide has receded, and the creatures crawl their way out of holes in the sand and scurry toward the water. The nightly ritual of waking and joining the sea. They cover the beach, making each step we take a risk. Step on a crab, risk a pinch. I look down at my bare feet, suddenly wishing I hadn't tossed my flip-flops off the second I hit sand.

Jeremiah notices. "I can carry you if you want." His feet are protected by thick leather sandals.

"Or we could wait."

He shrugs. "Up to you."

Of course, with Jeremiah, everything is up to me. I run my fingers up his arm. "Alright, I'll ride." Who can pass up the opportunity to grip those shoulders?

He kneels down, in perfect taekwondo warrior stance, and I climb onto his back, wrapping my arms around his neck and burrowing my face in his shoulder. He smells of sweat and the ocean, and that undeniable, perfect Jeremiah scent. I could smell that all day.

He grips my thighs and stands, then scoots forward, eyes pinned on the ground where he steps around scurrying crabs, careful not to crush them. I close my eyes so only the light of the moon shines through, and I let the gentle rocking of his movements and the sound of the waves breaking on the shore lull me to a half-sleep.

Then he stops in front of the remnants of the bonfire. "We're here."

I peer over his shoulder. Shelby and Miles are fooling around in the shadows, and a dozen other college-aged students are lounging around the weak flames in various states of drunkenness and undress. I don't want to be in this crowd. Not right now, when the world is perfect.

"Can't you just carry me all the way back to the car?" I murmur.

I can almost hear the smile playing at his lips. "For you, Dani? Anything."

Last Quarter

Jeremiah's parents have to work on Labor Day, so he's stuck at home babysitting his brothers and sisters. He offers to let me come over and help, but I didn't feel like wading my way through a sea of screaming children just to be with my boyfriend.

"I might just hang out with Shelby," I say over the phone, "We haven't really gotten to girl talk much lately."

I can hear Jeremiah shuffling around in the background, clearly distracted.

"Sounds good, I'll see ya tomorrow."

There's a loud thump, and he hurries to say goodbye then hangs up before telling me that he loves me, which is a little out of the ordinary, but he's got his hands full. And who could doubt how he feels after last Friday night?

Technically, I'm grounded for staying out too late Friday night, but Mom's also at work so there's no way she can enforce it. As long as I'm home before her, I'm okay.

When I get to Shelby's house, she's already swimming laps in her family's pool. When she sees me, she swims over and folds her arms on the wall. "You better have brought a swimsuit, because I'm spending the entire day in the pool. Mom's having the pool boy close it up tonight."

I grin. "Got it on under my clothes." I peel my clothes off and toss them on one of the lounge chairs, then dive into the cool water. It's not swimming in the ocean, but it's the next best thing. I turn a few somersaults in the water, then surface. I swim over to the edge of the pool to lounge with Shelby. "Have I ever told you how lucky you are to have your own pool?"

"Only about a thousand times."

"Well you are." I push hair out of my eyes. "The neighborhood pool is always so full of moms with their little kids and weird middle school boys who are always looking at me all creepy like."

Shelby laughs. "Gross."

"Yeah," I agree, "I'm never wearing that two piece you made me buy ever again."

"Did you at least try it on for Jeremiah?"

Then suddenly I realize, between Shelby being out of town all summer and school starting, I never really had a chance to tell her. "Actually, yeah."

"Did he like it?" The conspiratorial gleam in her eye tells me she already knows the answer.

"Yes!"

"Oh my God! You didn't!"

I nod my head. "Yes, we did!"

Shelby squeals. Like actually squeals. And pulls me into a hug. "Dani, I am so proud of you! My little girl all grown up into a real woman now!" She squeezes me then lets me go. "Tell me everything! Where did you do it? What was it like?"

"Uh… my bedroom." I bite my lip. "It was good, I guess. I uh… laughed at him."

Shelby's face dropped. "What?!"

I shrug. "Well, we had just finished, and he was trying to be all cutesy and romantic and he said I was beautiful."

"Aw, that's so sweet." Shelby leans back on the wall and sighs. "Whenever Miles is done, he just says he's hungry and heads to the kitchen."

I wrinkly my nose but don't say anything. Sometimes, with Shelby it's better not to compare lifestyles.

"So," she says, dropping the wistful look and getting back to the gossip, "how many times have you done it?"

"Three."

She cocks her head, waiting for more details.

I continue, "twice that day, then again at the beach on Friday."

"Oooh, beach sex, nice! Very romantic."

"It was," I sigh. "It was perfect." I feel a twinge in the space between my legs just thinking about it—Jeremiah and me and the waves.

Then Shelby pulls me straight out of my daydream with one simple comment. "Still, seems weird that he's letting whole weeks go by without jumping on you."

My mouth drops open, and I lick my lips quickly to cover for the initial shock. "We've just been struggling to get some alone time. That's all."

"Uh huh," she says dismissively. "He has a car, right? Can't be that hard to find a place to park it."

"Jeremiah wouldn't like that." He wouldn't. The cramped space, the feeling that we could be caught at any time. That's not his style. He likes things neat and tidy.

Shelby shrugs. "Suit yourself. Just know that once you give a guy sex, you have to keep at it, or he'll find it somewhere else."

And just like that, my perfect memory of that night at the beach with Jeremiah feels a little less perfect.

Shelby can tell she's upset me. She throws an arm over my shoulder. "I'm sure it's like you said. Having a hard time getting away from the parents. Don't get so upset. Jeremiah loves you."

"Yeah," I whisper, "he does."

"See? No big deal." Then she pushes off from the wall. "Besides, you came over to swim, so let's swim."

Last Quarter

Grounded means no Jeremiah. Mom drives me to school, and she's waiting there to pick me up as soon as it lets out. I spend the rest of the afternoon at her work, a non-profit called Earth's Bounty which works to provide clean water to third-world countries. If I have enough homework, I can work on that in her office, under her watchful eye. On days when I'm short the homework, I have to help with her work. Which basically means filing.

So much filing.

Mountains of filing.

One thing I've learned from all this experience, whatever job I do end up doing when I join the workforce, I sure hope it doesn't include filing.

The only time I get to see Jeremiah or Shelby is at school. Which is great, but it's not enough. Jeremiah feels horrible that I got grounded, but I don't. To me, it was worth it. A thousand times worth it. Because I've never felt closer to him. It's like that night turned us into more than simply boyfriend and girlfriend.

I try to explain it to Shelby in Wednesday gym class, but she doesn't get it.

"So, you had great sex?" she pants out, as we turn the corner for our fourth lap in the mile run. "Big deal."

"No, it was more than that." I pick up the pace to keep up with her. Shelby's got natural endurance, but I feel like I'm about to die. I'm not out of shape or anything, I'm just not a runner like she is. "Jeremiah and me… I dunno. I can't explain it. It's just…"

"Great sex at the beach, under the moonlight." She does a half-hearted wave of her hands around her head, like she's cheering sarcastically for something.

"Fine, whatever. Just forget about it."

"What?" she says with a mocking pout. "I'm happy for you."

"Yeah, you sound really happy."

Shelby rolls her eyes. "Sometimes, it just gets really boring listening to you go on and on about your perfect boyfriend. Like you think you're the first girl ever to have a great time with her guy? Get over yourself, Dani."

She picks up the pace to sprint the last 100 meters to the finish line. There's no way I can keep up. I cross the finish line well behind her, then double over.

"Nine minutes, thirty-five seconds, Miller." Coach Wilson barely glances up from his stopwatch.

I gasp for breath. A personal best, but that's just because I was trying to keep pace with Shelby. My heart feels like it's about to explode out of my chest, and I can't calm it. Maybe I overdid it, running so hard.

I stretch to my full height to suck in more air, and my chest feels tight. I can feel my heart racing, my pulse drums in my ears and I'm lightheaded. I start to gasp. Is this what a heart attack feels like? I can't breathe.

Shelby notices first. She grabs my elbow. "Walk. You have to walk it off." She would know. She's been in track and cross-country every year since we started high school.

I start to pace with her, but I can't. My legs don't seem to be working right. I collapse to the ground and put my head between my knees. "My chest…" I gasp. "It hurts…"

Shelby grabs my wrist. "Your pulse is racing."

I know. I can feel it.

By now the whole class is gathered around me. I wish I could dig a hole and crawl into it. There's nothing worse than having eyes on you.

Coach Wilson saunters over, clearly unperturbed that one of his students is about to die on the football field. "What's going on?"

Shelby speaks for me. "She can't cool down."

"Walk it off, Miller."

I shake my head and clutch my chest with my free hand. "Can't…"

He kneels next to me with a grunt. "How do you feel?"

"Dizzy," I say between gasps.

"Lay back," he orders. "Take deep breaths."

I do what he says, and it starts to work. While I watch clouds float across the sky, he barks orders at the rest of the class to start hiking back inside. Shelby stays with me, her hand still around my wrist. Comforting enough that I forget to be mad at her for her comment about Jer and me.

"Are you okay?" she asks.

"Cerulean," I murmur.

"What?"

"It's the color of the sky." I point up lazily. "Isn't it beautiful?"

She snorts and pulls me to my feet. "You are so weird."

I'm still a little dizzy, so I lean on Shelby as we walk back to the school.

Coach meets us at the gate. "How are you feeling?"

"Better."

He nods. "You're probably just coming down with a cold or something. Take it easy for the rest of the day. Make sure you drink plenty of water."

I don't know. I've never had a cold that made me feel like this.

New Moon

Literally, the only thing in the world that can get me out of being grounded and trapped at home with my mom is court ordered quality time with my dad. It's like having to choose whether I want my fingernails yanked or my eyes gouged. Which form of torture is best?

Dad waits for me on the front porch. He hasn't set foot in our house since the divorce, at least not that I can remember. Not that Mom has specifically forbidden him, it's just understood. No Dad in the house.

Mom fusses with me in the foyer, so I'm trapped in the doorway between the two of them. "Have fun," she says as she hands me my jacket, then she looks at Dad. "Remember, she's grounded, so try not to spoil her."

"So much for having fun," I mumble.

She glares at me. "Don't test me, Dani. I can add another week."

"Sorry."

Dad leans on the door frame. "Lighten up, Hannah. It's not like you never snuck out of the house with your boyfriend when you were her age."

My ears perk up. Mom and Dad sneaking around back when they actually liked each other? Mom sees my expression and her jaw clenches. "Well, look how that turned out." She shoves me toward the door. "Have her back by nine. She has chores tomorrow, and I don't want her too tired to do them."

Dad throws up a mock salute. "Yes, Sarge!"

He's lucky he's out of arm's reach, because Mom looks ready to throw punches. Instead, she slams the door, leaving the two of us alone on the steps.

"C'mon Dani-lion," Dad says, "Ashley's waiting in the car."

"Too scared to walk up to the front door?" I ask sarcastically.

He chuckles. "Something like that."

It feels good, making fun of Ashley with Dad, but then I start to think about how I would feel if Jeremiah made fun of me behind my back. I don't get how Dad can be like that. Joking around with people one second and sneering at them behind their backs the next.

I wonder what he says about me to Ashley when I'm not around. Or about Mom.

Probably that I'm surly and she's a bitch. Maybe he thinks I'm a disappointment. My stomach drops.

"I was thinking we'd get burgers before we bowl?" Dad suggests, breaking my train of thought.

"Sure, yeah."

Ashley is about three quarters of the way through her cigarette when we arrive at the car. She flicks it onto our front lawn when she sees us approaching, and in spite of myself, I wrinkle my nose. Mom will die when she sees a cigarette butt in her grass, and a part of me wants to yell at her to pick it up. But the other part of me thinks I'll just sound like Mom if I do, and the thought of turning into Mom makes me want to puke.

* * *

Dad is super competitive when it comes to bowling. He's bowled a three hundred on multiple occasions. Perfect game. It's nice because it means when we have our family bowling nights, he doesn't bother to keep up the conversation. He's too busy manning the scoreboard. Ashley tries for a little while, asking about school and Jeremiah, but after a few frames, she gives up, and between my turns, I can hide in the corner and play on my phone.

That is until I see Mr. Craig across the alley with his family. At least, I assume it's his family. Two kids, elementary school aged, with the same reddish-brown hair he has, and a pretty wife. They're not ignoring each other, like my family is. They're laughing and high-fiving. His wife bowls a strike and literally leaps into his arms. Like actually leaps. If I tried that with Jeremiah at school, he'd write me up for PDA so fast.

I lift my phone to snap a picture and post on Instagram, but he sees me. Looks directly at my camera. I gulp.

He disentangles himself from his wife and makes his away across the alley to me. "Danielle Miller!" he says when he reaches the booth where I'm sitting.

I sink lower and pray for spontaneous combustion. "Hey."

Dad turns around. "Dani? Who's this?"

"Dad, Mr. Craig," I mumble as I wave my hand at each of them. "Mr. Craig, my dad."

Mr. Craig holds out his hand. "Nice to meet you. I've got Danielle for Creative Writing this year, and homeroom! Doubly lucky." And laying it on thick. I roll my eyes.

Dad shakes his hand. "Good to meet you." His name is flashing on the TV screen, saying it's his turn, and he's itching to throw a ball.

Ashley comes up behind him, just finishing her round.

"Ah," Mr. Craig says, "you must be Danielle's mom!"

He really stepped in it this time. How he thinks Ashley is even remotely old enough to have a teenage daughter. Well, she'd had to have had me at like sixteen. I burst into laughter as Ashley stutters, "oh, no… no, that's um, I mean I uh…"

"She's my dad's girlfriend." I say, emphasizing the girlfriend. Not a fiancée. Not a wife.

"Oh, well, I beg your pardon," Mr. Craig says. He doesn't even look embarrassed about his mistake. "Well, as I was saying. I'm Danielle's Creative Writing teacher. She shows a lot of promise, let me tell you."

In spite of myself, I look up from behind my phone. Dad strolls over after throwing yet another strike.

"Promise, huh?" he asks.

"Oh yes," Mr. Craig says, "just last week, she turned in a poem that was very," he pauses and looks at me, "eye opening."

Now all three of them are looking at me. "Poetry, huh?" Dad asks, grinning. He thinks it's a joke.

I shrug. "I think it's my turn to bowl."

Mr. Craig nods. "Well, good seeing you." He shakes my dad's hand then turns to leave. "Oh, and Danielle?"

"Yeah?"

"Delete that picture. I don't want my children on your social media. Got it?" The raised eyebrow and folded arms leave no room for argument.

"Yeah, uh, sorry."

By the time I return to my seat, Mr. Craig has left. But my dad is still looking at me like he found out some dirty secret. He just can't stop laughing.

Waxing Crescent

Saturday morning, Mom barrels into my room at the crack of dawn with a voice too cheery for words and hair already styled to perfection.

"Wake up, sleepyhead!" she sings as she yanks open my curtains. "Don't you know what day it is?"

"The day I get thrown in prison for murdering my mom?" I grumble as I stretch.

She turns and frowns at me. "No," she says, all the previous joy in her voice vanishes. "It's our annual luncheon."

I groan. How did I forget? Once a year, my mom's charity does this huge luncheon fundraiser. Everyone who works at Earth's Bounty makes a dish, though Mom always goes above and beyond and makes three, then anyone who wants a plate just has to pay twenty bucks to get in. Practically everyone in town shows up, largely in part because Mom makes blackberry cobbler that would make Betty Crocker herself jealous.

And in the middle of it all, I get roped into helping. I have to help make food, then dress in my nicest dress, the sort I would have to wear to church if I went to church, and put on an apron and dish congealed macaroni and cheese to anyone who comes through the line.

Mom is already out my bedroom door by the time I plant my feet on the ground. She's downstairs pulling the cobbler out of the oven as I trudge to the bathroom. I catch a whiff of the bubbling sweet dish and my stomach turns.

"Do you want me to fix breakfast?" Mom calls up the stairs.

I clench my jaw shut and breathe through my nose as my stomach churns again, and all I can think of is Coach Wilson saying that maybe I was coming down with something, but that was over a week ago. I should feel better by now, right? I turn and run for the bathroom.

"Dani?"

I can hear Mom's footsteps on the stairs.

"You okay?"

I break out into a cold sweat, and blood rushes to my ears. I can't tell if I'm going to throw up or not. I snatch a towel from the shelf above the toilet and run some cold water over it, before pressing the icy fabric to my face.

That's better. I can breathe again.

Mom appears in the doorway. "What's going on?"

"I think I'm sick."

"I would say so."

I shiver, the wave of heat from only a minute earlier has given way, and suddenly I'm freezing. I don't want to say it. What we're both thinking. If I'm sick, I can't serve food. Health hazard. But if I say it, she'll think I'm trying to get out of helping. She has to be the one.

She stares at me, leaning over the sink, for several long seconds, then she lets out a long, dramatic sigh. "I guess you're too sick to work the luncheon then." She doesn't sound like she believes me.

"I'm sorry." Neither of us really believes that.

She purses her lips, like I've personally offended her. Like I did this on purpose to get out of working with her. Then she nods once, turns on her heel, and heads back to the kitchen. "Back to bed then. I'll make you some broth."

* * *

Mom still goes to the luncheon. She kind of has to, since she runs the charity and all, so I stay home by myself with some homemade soup and Netflix. Honestly, I feel kind of bad, because after the initial rush to the bathroom, my stomach seems to have calmed down. I don't even really feel sick anymore.

So I write a note to her to let her know where I'm heading, then bike over to see Granny. Might as well hang out with her, since Shelby and Jeremiah are off limits. I'm getting bored by myself.

This time, Granny's definitely having a good day. She has her knitting in her lap and she loops yarn over her needles while I braid her hair into a thick French braid, and wind it around her head.

"You look like a queen," I say when I'm finished, and she smiles.

"You're so sweet, Dani."

"Tell Mom that," I mutter as I take my seat across from her.

Granny keeps knitting, humming a little to herself. "Be gentle with your mother. She's been through a lot."

"I know."

I must not sound like I do, because Granny's eyes meet mine, then turn to the window. "Look out there, Dani. What do you see?"

"I don't know," I say. "A parking lot. Trees."

"And what color are these trees?"

I raise an eyebrow and look back at her, but she nods again to the window.

"Um, well it's fall, so the leaves are all changing. Some of them are still green, but about half are red or yellow."

"Mm hmm," Granny says with a nod. "Don't you see?"

"See what?"

She sets down her knitting and leans forward, gripping my hand. "Every year, the seasons change. The weather turns cold, the leaves fall, but they come back again in the spring. Life renews."

"Okay…" I'm not sure where this is going.

"Mother Nature has her cycles. She gives, and she takes. She can be harsh, like all women, but caring and nurturing as well. Nature took something very dear from your mom, from all of us. But like all women, we are strong. We persevere. Your mom works hard to take care of you, to give you a good life."

My stomach churns with guilt over how I've been acting. "I know."

Granny nods and sits back. "We all have our difficulties, Dani. But in the end, it balances out. The good and the bad. The giving and the taking. And when all is said and done, what we create is something beautiful. Yes, it is."

Her eyelids droop a little, the knitting lays forgotten on her lap.

"You really believe that?" I ask.

She sighs. "For women, yes."

"And for men?"

"Men are like the sun. You spend too much time with them, you'll get burned."

First Quarter

"Let's talk poetry." Mr. Craig's earnest gaze lands on me and I swear, if I murdered him right now, it would be completely justified.

"Few written forms offer the same freedom, the same opportunities for raw, soul-bearing expression that poetry does. The art and choice of form, the symbolism. Yes, these belong to all forms of written word, but none so much as poetry."

He grabs a stack of papers off his desk. "Consider this. Every March, our school hosts the annual Poetry Slam, and every year, my Creative Writing students exceed expectations, nay, dare I say, blow the roof off the auditorium with the power of their words?" He pauses for emphasis and grins at the class. "I'll admit, it's become a point of pride."

"This year, I expect no different," he says as he hands papers around the classroom, "and because I expect only the best, and because, like all forms of art, true poetic genius only comes after hours upon hours of practice," he pauses and drops the last paper on my desk, "I've decided to start our poetry unit early."

"Every two weeks, we will explore a new theme, be it desire or pain, love or loss. Something that speaks to us at our very cores. We will free write, we will comb through our words, searching for only those that burn us with their sheer intensity, and we will commit them to paper, hone them, make them do our bidding, and then…" He's made his way to the front of the classroom and throws his arms wide to get our attention. "Then, my brilliant young minds, we will stand before our brethren and speak our truths with passion, with feeling, with—"

"What does that even mean?" someone asks from the back.

Mr. Craig's arm drops to the side, clearly hurt that someone dared interrupt his speech.

"It means," he says dryly, "that you'll be reading your poetry to the class to critique."

Cue the collective groan.

***

Shelby barrels into me in the hallway between third and fourth periods. "Don't shut your—"

Too late, the locker door was already swinging shut before I saw her.

Her shoulders slump. "—locker."

"Sorry."

She doesn't acknowledge the apology, just launches straight into her request. "I need a tampon."

I cringe. "I don't have any."

"Really?" she says with a quirk of the eyebrow. "You always have tampons."

True. I usually keep a supply because I'm horribly irregular and it's better to have them when you don't need them than to waddle to the nurse's office when you do.

I apologize again. "I just haven't needed them yet this year."

Shelby stops walking and grabs my arm. "Never? We've been in school for like…" she pauses and counts on her fingers. "Five weeks."

"So?"

She's giving me a look like I've grown a third arm or something. "Well, you should have had something by now."

"I'm hard to predict," I argue. "It's not like a set schedule."

"Do you remember when your last one was?"

I try to think. "Not really."

Shelby pulls me closer and leans in to whisper in my ear. "Are you sure you're not pregnant?"

I yank my arm away. "Geez, Shelby. Of course not!"

"Okay," she looks doubtful. "Just, you said you and Jeremiah…" her voice trails off.

I roll my eyes. "I'm not…" I glance around then mouth the word, *pregnant*. "I'm probably just stressed with school and stuff. People skip all the time. It's not a big deal."

"If you say so."

"I do," I say firmly.

That settles the matter. Or it should have, except all through fourth hour, all I can think about is trying to figure out when my last period was. And then, I start to hear Mom's nagging voice in the back of my head, telling me to keep track on the calendar app on my phone. "It's part of being a woman, Dani. You'll have fewer accidents if you learn to predict it."

I never really cared about it before. Now, I spend all Chemistry class racking my brain trying to remember and I'm coming up with only one possibility.

The first week of August.

That can't be right. That's like seven weeks ago! Surely, I've had something since then. I'm irregular, but I've never gone that long without a period.

My heart starts to race, and once it starts, it can't stop. This can't be right.

Except, we didn't use a condom. Not that first time.

But, what are the chances of getting pregnant on one try? I'm pretty sure we covered this in Health class freshman year. God, why didn't I pay attention? Because I didn't think I'd need to.

Plus, it wasn't one try. It was two.

Still… it seems pretty unlikely.

My heart is about ready to leap out of my chest and I lean over my desk, groaning. No, please, please God, no.

"Ms. Miller," Mrs. Humphries says sternly. "Please sit up."

I do, but only barely. "Can I go to the nurse? I feel sick." As soon as I say it, I can feel the acid bubbling up in my stomach, and I can taste vomit in the back of my throat.

Nope. I have to get out of this classroom. Mrs. Humphries hasn't answered me yet, but I'm already out the door, racing down the hall. Oh, it's coming.

It's…

I double over. I haven't made it into the bathroom yet, but it's too late. My breakfast splatters all over the linoleum floor outside of the girl's restroom. I heave again, emptying my stomach. Then, I start to cry.

I don't even know why. Maybe I'm just embarrassed, or maybe it's the final proof I needed. First the racing pulse in gym class, then the queasiness over my mom's cobbler. Now this.

I sink to the floor next to my pile of vomit and sob.

I probably would have stayed there all hour, but some underclassmen walks out of the bathroom and just about slides across the hallway in my pile of filth. Lucky for me, she's sweet about it. Some people would have only focused on their own inconvenience, but she just sidesteps the mess and kneels down beside me.

"Are you okay?"

Kind of a stupid question, considering, but I don't have it in me to argue, so I just shake my head through my tears.

"I'll go get the nurse, okay?" She darts off, and within minutes returns with Nurse Flores, who I'm pretty sure lives for these sorts of days.

She actually looks excited with her floral print scrubs and her dark hair in a tight bun. She tucks an arm under my armpits and lifts me up. "Come on, sweetie. Let's get you to the clinic."

I cast one final look at the puddle of vomit on the floor. Is it too much to hope this isn't happening to me?

My legs wobble as we make our way down the hallway, like they'll barely hold me up. It's some sort of miracle I even make it to the nurse's clinic before collapsing into the chair.

"Now," she says, bustling around the room grabbing a thermometer and a blood pressure cuff. "Let's see what's going on with you."

I accept the thermometer in my mouth without argument and stare into space as she checks my heart rate and blood pressure.

"Blood pressure seems normal. Heart rate is a little high." She yanks the thermometer out of my mouth. "No temperature. Hmm."

"Uh," I mumble.

"Yes?" She stops and fixes me with a hawk-like stare.

"Do you have a… um…" Do I really have to say this out loud?

She raises an eyebrow questioningly.

Yes, apparently, I do. "A um… pregnancy test?" It comes out at barely a squeak. I can't even look at her while I say it. I stare at my feet.

"Oh." She turns back to bustle around in the cabinet behind her desk then comes back with a long thin test wrapped in thick pink plastic. She hands it to me without a word, her face reveals nothing about what she's thinking. The height of professionalism.

The moment of truth. I look up. "How does it work?" How many times has she had to deal with a scared teen girl in her office?

She takes a breath and flips the package over in my hand. "Look. You pee on that end there, then wait for a couple minutes. There's a chemical in it that will react if you're pregnant. One pink line means no pregnancy. Two means you are."

I don't move. I just stare at the test in my hands, and everything feels suddenly so real and so surreal at the same time. The whole world is spinning, and I'm stuck in this place. Neither here nor there, but on the precipice between.

She nods toward the bathroom door connected to her office. "Take all the time you need."

I close my eyes and count to ten, but my heart is still beating rapidly, so I keep counting. I get to twenty, then thirty, then on. By the time I reach forty-seven, I'm ready. I stand and make my way to the bathroom. A single person set up at the back of the nurse's office. It smells strongly of anti-septic, and I wonder if someone else has already puked in there today. Then, when I think about it, I start to feel like I'm going to throw up again, so I push the idea out of my mind.

Everything feels heavy and slow, and I get that feeling of being there, but not really there. Of watching from the outside. Each step of the way. I unzip my jeans and push them down around my ankles, then sit on the stool, reaching awkwardly between my legs with the test. I can't seem to get a stream going. Pure stage fright. I start thinking about the nurse in the adjacent office knowing exactly what I'm doing, then I think about Shelby's look of superiority, and about what it will be like, actually being pregnant. It's a rabbit hole, plain and simple. Once I start thinking about it, I can't stop.

I have thought about having kids with Jeremiah. Just, in my dreams, I imagine us about ten years older, married and working and, well… adults. Not like this.

Well, I'm never going to start peeing if I keep this up, so I reach over and turn on the faucet. Then I close my eyes and start reciting poetry under my breath. It's a silly habit I picked up a few years ago. My mom's suggestion, because I had trouble relaxing in crowded bathrooms. She said to just start reciting something I have memorized, and that will put my mind off of what's happening around me.

I've always been good at memorizing poetry. What can I say? It's my thing.

And it does the trick. About halfway through Emily Dickinson's *There came a day at summer's full,* the pee starts flowing. And of course, since women's bodies aren't exactly made for aiming, I wind up getting it all over my hand and very little on the stick itself.

I get enough though, because I can already see the stick absorbing the liquid. And pretty soon, the first line beings to appear. One line though. That's nothing.

Then, the second line appears.

It's not even faint. Like, if it were faint enough, maybe I could tell myself there's been some mistake.

No, it's a bright pink angry line that can only mean one thing.

I'm pregnant.

"Oh God," I whisper. "Please… no…"

Of course, according to Granny, God is a man, and therefore not a good listener. It all makes sense.

While I'm having these sacrilegious thoughts about why God is a man, and simultaneously trying to process the idea that I'm pregnant—like really, honest to goodness, growing a human being inside my body pregnant—I'm also sitting on a toilet with my underwear around my ankles. I mean, I haven't even wiped yet.

I probably would have sat there forever, but the nurse knocks on the door. "Are you alright in there?"

That spurs me into action. I start to throw the test in the trashcan, then I have the ridiculous notion that someone will use this bathroom after me, and possibly find it, and know I was in there, and put two and two together…

So instead, I wrap it in toilet paper and shove it in my bag. Then I holler at the door. "Yeah, I'm fine. Just finishing up."

I hastily wipe and flush the toilet, then wash my hands. Hovering over the sink, I take several long deep breaths, until the redness in my face has gone down and I look calm and normal.

The nurse looks up as I exit the bathroom. "How are you feeling?"

"Alright." I pause. "Um, it came back negative."

"That's good, but you threw up, so I have to send you home."

"Okay."

I'm flabbergasted that she's so calm. Girl comes in, asks for a pregnancy test, and she's sitting there writing a pass on a Post-It note.

"Do you need a ride home?" she asks, "I can call your mom."

I shake my head automatically, even though I don't have a car or a license. I can't see my mom right now.

She hands me the pass. "Try to take it easy."

"Thanks," I mutter. Fat chance.

I start walking to the front door, figuring I'll just walk home and the time on my feet will give me a chance to clear my head, but I have to pass through the hallway of senior lockers to get there, and as I pass Jeremiah's, I stop.

This is crazy. But I need space and time to clear my head, and he has a car.

I spin the lock on Jeremiah's locker. I know the combination, of course. Jer and I don't keep secrets. He knows mine as well. Sometimes, he even leaves presents inside. A bar of chocolate or a flower or something. He's real sweet like that.

I'm don't leave anything for Jeremiah. Instead, I take something away. I rummage around in the pockets on his jacket until I find his car keys.

"Please don't be mad," I whisper.

I'm treading in shark-infested waters now. I pocket the keys, then shut the locker and head for the doors to the student parking lot. Shoving them open, I step out into the crisp late October air. Freedom.

Jeremiah parks in the same spot every single day, and I head straight for his car. Once in the driver's seat, I pause. Jer lets me drive occasionally, even though I don't have my license. I'm used to his car. It's familiar. I'm actually a pretty good driver, I just stress out when my mom rides with me. She has a way of second-guessing everything I do, and I get flustered and make dumb mistakes. Which she of course takes to mean that I need more practice, which means more time with her, which means more mistakes.

It's a vicious cycle.

Without her, I'm fine.

As if to prove it, I turn the key and his engine roars to life.

This is insane. Absolutely insane.

I back the car out of the space, pull onto the street, and drive. I hop on the first highway ramp I can find, and I keep driving. At some point, my phone starts ringing, and instead of answering, I shut it off.

I don't even know where I'm going until the exit options run out and I'm facing water.

Langley Beach.

Granny brought me here every summer since I was born. Then just a few weeks ago, Jeremiah brought me here too. Was that when it happened?

I park the car and stumble toward the water. The news really hits me when I'm ankle deep in the ocean.

Pregnant.

My brain races a mile a minute. How could I be pregnant? Why is this happening to me? What did I do wrong?

Am I being punished?

The salt water dances around my ankles, splashing up my legs and soaking through my jeans. I pull the test out of my purse and look again. Sure enough, two pink lines. There's no doubt about it.

I'm pregnant.

The tears I've been holding back since I first saw the test result start to flow. Oh God. I can't. I can't do this. I long to press the looped arrow on the YouTube video of my life and just start over. I don't need to have my life planned out to Mom's standards to know that this is derailing everything.

I fall to my knees and the water splashes against my hips, cold and jarring. My jacket feels heavy, and I know I should worry about how the salt in the water will ruin the fabric. But it seems like such a minuscule thing to care about, when the fabric of my life is literally unraveling around me.

I double over and scream. Half scream, half sob. I can't hold back. Every emotion I've been holding onto since I found out comes bursting forth.

"How could you do this to me?" I screech into the wind, not even sure who I'm talking to. Then I bellow incoherently. The primal, guttural cry of a wounded animal. That's how I feel. Wounded.

The screams subside into crying, and as the tide comes in, I crawl higher on the beach, away from the water. I sit on the sand and watch the waves come in and retreat. The calming ebb and flow of waves. I time my breaths with the waves, come in, go out, breathe in, breathe out. Like the yoga Granny used to practice every morning, with five-year-old me pretending to follow along. I like the predictability of the waves. I like that I know exactly what will happen at any given moment. Not like my life.

It's too late in the season for any tourists, and for most of the afternoon, I have the beach to myself. What visitors who do come walk past me without a second glance. Maybe I look homeless.

Eventually, I stop crying, but I don't leave. I sit there with my arms wrapped around my knees and continue to watch the water. I want something. Proof that I'll be okay. Proof that I can get through this. The ocean offers nothing, just the same old rise and fall of waves on sand.

I sit there until the moon comes out. It comes early, the sky has not yet darkened. The moon is waxing, growing, getting bigger, but not yet full. Like me.

Granny says the moon is a woman. She is born, she grows beautiful, she grows heavy with child, then she grows old and bent, and eventually disappears. Then she starts again. The life cycle of the moon is one month. Lucky her. For real women, it takes significantly longer.

I can hear Granny's patient voice in my head as she explains her silly theories. God is a man, because he does not listen, and I have to agree with her there. The sun is a man, because he is so demanding. But the Earth is a woman, and the moon her daughter.

"You can tell," pretend Granny says, "because they take what the Sun forces upon them, and they turn it into something beautiful. The Earth," she says, "creates life. Only a woman can do that."

"And the moon?" I ask.

"Creates beauty."

I imagine her cupping my chin as she says this and lifting it higher. Reminding me that I am a woman, and should be proud and hold myself up to the Moon's standard at every second. "The Moon reflects the Sun's light, but she is beautiful. You cannot look at the Sun, because he is so harsh, so unkind. The Moon takes what is unkind and makes it soft and gentle."

At this point, I don't even know what's nonsense and what's real. The sun and the moon and the earth are grand objects, and I am just one human beneath the sky, trying to make do with what I have. One human who just wants to live her life.

But if the moon can turn pain into beauty, maybe so can I.

* * *

When I climb into Jeremiah's car to drive home, I turn my phone back on and find about thirty missed phone calls. Most of them from my mom, but also a few from Dad and Jeremiah, and even one from Shelby. Add to that the text messages; I have never seen the little red icon get so high. Who knew it went into triple digits?

I take a deep breath then pull the car out of the lot. Then, I dial Mom's phone number.

She picks up on the first ring. "Dani? Where are you?"

"I'm—"

But she doesn't let me finish. "I've been worried sick. Do you have any clue what it's like to have your daughter just disappear from school?"

"Mom, I'm—"

"Your nurse calls, tells me you're sick and you've signed out, then three hours later, Jeremiah tells me you took his car? You don't even have a license! Do you understand what sort of trouble you could get into? What the hell is wrong with you?"

"Mom—"

"Jeremiah's sitting here crying, thinking that he's done something wrong."

"Is he mad?" I whisper.

I can hear her breathing heavily on the other end. "Is he mad? Of course, he is. We're all mad, Dani! We're all thinking that you've gotten yourself into some sort of trouble, worried you might be hurt, or… or…" Her voice cracks, and I suddenly feel so awful.

"I'm sorry."

"Damn right, you're sorry," she hisses. "Get your ass home. Now."

I nod, even though I know she can't hear a nod. "Okay." My voice cracks, but she doesn't seem to care. She hangs up, and I'm left to drive home in silence. I spend the time praying I don't get pulled over, because getting in trouble with the law would be the absolute last straw for me at this point.

Mom hates me. How could she not? What kind of person does this? Just steals a car and ditches town for half a day. I wonder if she's going to kick me out. I could see it. This might be it for us. Things have never been good between us, but I could see her deciding that she's had enough. Maybe she'll make me live with my dad. It wouldn't be the worst thing in the world, except I really don't like Ashley.

I just don't see how I can come back from this.

And Jeremiah. Poor Jeremiah. He's going to break up with me. I would, if the tables were turned. Even though I love him. I stole his car, I ditched him. I broke into his locker and took his keys and left town without even a word to him.

And I'm pregnant.

I feel like I'm driving toward my life sentence. No more Mom. No more Jeremiah. I'll be all alone. At least for the next several months. Then I'll be alone with a baby.

I cry most of the drive home. I thought I had finished crying at the beach, but I was wrong. I pass exit after exit with tears in my eyes, dripping down my chin and onto my lap. I'm not even sure if I'm crying over losing my mom, or Jeremiah, or because I'm losing myself. No more Dani Miller. Pretty soon, I'll just be a loser teen mom. The kind of girls Shelby used to laugh at freshman year, struggling their way through school.

It's past dark when I pull into the driveway. The lights are on. Jeremiah's parents' car is sitting in the driveway, and so is my dad's. Ashley leans against the front porch smoking a cigarette. And even though I'm walking toward my own doom, I can't help but think that it's funny that even in the middle of all this, Mom still makes Ashley go outside to smoke.

I see her duck into the house as I park the car in the driveway. Seconds later, Mom bursts through the front door and sprints to the car. I've only barely climbed out when she yanks me into a bone-crushing hug.

"Ow, Mom!"

"Shh…" She squeezes harder and I can feel her whole body shaking. Then I recognize the sound in my ear. She's sobbing. I thought she'd hate me forever. But she's just holding me and bawling her eyes out.

"I'm sorry," I whisper.

"I know," she says, "I know."

* * *

By some miracle, she doesn't ground me. Probably because the minutes that follow our reunion are some of the longest in my life. Mom wraps her arm around my shoulders and all but drags me into the house. Everyone is standing in the foyer, and not just my parents and Jeremiah, but his parents too. Everyone has come out to see Dani Miller get hers.

Jeremiah refuses to look at me. Or if he does glance my way, it's always when I don't see. Even if we did make eye contact, we'd never have a chance to talk. Everyone is crowding around me, wanting to know why I left, where I went, everything.

Dad keeps saying that he was "so worried" but that's bullshit, because his hand is on Ashley's waist and they keep whispering to each other and smiling every time they think no one is watching. How they don't notice Mom's seething glare is beyond me.

On top of that, Jeremiah's parents are clearly pissed. They usher him out of the door as fast as they can without saying anything to me. Instead, his mom just holds out her hand to me, silently demanding his car keys back.

I pull them out of my pocket and drop them gently into her palm. "I'm sorry."

But she doesn't respond. Instead, she frowns and steers Jeremiah out the front door.

"Jer?" I ask, looking past her, but he just shrugs and stares at the floor, and I feel like the biggest failure in the history of the world.

His mom pulls him along. "Come on, Jeremiah."

It hurts that she doesn't even seem to care. She and I have always gotten along so well, but now I'm just the screwed-up girl who stole her son's car.

I sigh.

Once Jeremiah and his parents leave, Dad sticks around for a little. Enough to say he's glad I'm safe and kiss me awkwardly on my head. "I'll see you Friday, Dani-lion."

Then it's just mom and me. I expect her to turn on me, to demand to know where I went or why. But instead, she just pulls me into another tight hug. "I'm just happy you're back."

And she really means it.

First Quarter

In spite of the late night, I wake up early the next morning. Or rather, my finicky stomach wakes me up early. I can hear Mom already downstairs, bustling around the kitchen. She wakes up before anyone I've ever met. When I was little, I tried to beat her, to make her breakfast for Mother's Day, but she was already up and pouring pancake batter into the pan when I got there. Maybe she doesn't sleep. It wouldn't surprise me if she had some super power that gave her the ability to live without sleep. It would explain how she manages to do everything so perfectly all the time.

I spend a few minutes dry-heaving into the toilet. I'm trying to do it quietly so my mom can't hear. Nothing comes up, which I guess makes sense. I haven't eaten since lunch the day before. When I'm done, I stand up on wobbly legs and go to the sink.

I'm pregnant.

It's like it's real, but it's not real at the same time. It just seems like a mistake, or a joke. Ha ha, Dani got pregnant. But already, I feel like I can sense something different about my body. Like I can feel the blood pumping through my veins, my heart pounding as it churns it through.

I try to imagine what I'll look like in a few months when my stomach rounds out like a basketball. I've never been particularly vain, but I don't love the idea of blowing up like a beach ball.

Then again… there's always the other option. The abortion option. I could do that, and I would never have to tell Jeremiah or my mom or anyone. Except I have no idea how one even goes about doing that, and it's got to be expensive. Shelby might know, but then I'd have to tell Shelby.

I lift my shirt and rub my stomach, staring at my reflection. It still feels flat and smooth. But not for much longer.

I'm half-afraid Jeremiah won't want to drive me to school anymore. He might still be mad about the whole stealing the car situation. Apparently, Mom agrees, because the first thing she says when I come down the stairs is, "I can drive you to school if you want."

I chew my lip for a few seconds and check my phone. It's 6:57. Usually Jeremiah shows up right at seven. "Let's wait and see," I say, sinking into the chair across from her.

She jumps up. "Do you want something to eat?"

The mere mention of food makes my stomach flip. "No thanks."

By 7:04, I'm starting to worry. Not that I think Jeremiah would just dump me unceremoniously like that, but I've taken questionable relationship behavior to a whole new level.

As I'm about to admit defeat and ask Mom to drive me, the doorbell rings. We both breathe a sigh of relief. I rush to answer it, and there's Jeremiah, looking perfect. Just perfect.

"Hey," he says, "Sorry I'm late. My mom and I had a fight."

"Oh, why?"

He gives me a look.

"Oh, yeah," I look down. "Sorry."

"Don't be. She's being unreasonable. You made one mistake, and she's acting like you're the worst thing to ever happen to me."

Wait until she finds out the real story.

Jeremiah reaches down and grabs my hand. "You know I'm here for you, right? No matter what?"

I nod.

"You can tell me anything." He squeezes my hand.

I nod again. It's too hard to look up at him, to see the earnestness in his eyes. I can already feel a lump forming in my throat. "I'm just going through something right now."

"Is it your mom?"

I shake my head.

"Your dad?"

"No." I force myself to look at him. "It's just personal stuff. Me stuff. I'll tell you about it, I promise. I just need to find the right time." There are tears building in the corners of my eyes, and a couple escape, rolling down my cheeks.

Thankfully, that convinces him. He pulls me into a tight hug and whispers in my ear, "I'll love you no matter what, okay?"

I nod into his chest. He smells so good. I know it sounds weird, but his smell was the first thing I ever noticed about him. I sat behind him in Biology my freshman year, and he smelled divine. I fell in love with that smell before I ever learned his name. He would sink into the chair, and the air would shift around me, and suddenly I could smell *him*.

I'm going to miss that when he finds out my secret. When he decides I'm too much trouble to keep around.

Waning Gibbous

* * *

It's funny, the way the one second, I can forget entirely about the secret, then another it comes storming back. I sit in Homeroom, while Mr. Craig leads us through yet another community circle where we discuss our hopes and fears and dreams about our futures. I listen to the other juniors say which colleges they think they'll apply to, what they want to major in, and at first, I join in. Then it comes back to me.

I'm pregnant.

I might not be going to college in two years. I might be changing diapers instead.

All their worries seem so silly. This guy got into a fight with his step-dad again. That girl is thinking about quitting volleyball because she doesn't like the coach. Shelby makes the most hilarious faces from across the circle when no one else is looking. She pantomimes everybody's little worries for my amusement, so I sometimes have to bite my lip to keep from laughing. I appreciate it though, being able to focus on something light-hearted instead of my big secret.

"And what about you, Danielle?" Mr. Craig asks. "Is there a weight on your shoulders these days?"

Is there ever.

I shake my head and smile. "Nope, all good here."

"Last week, you mentioned the Fall Bake Sale?" he presses.

Oh boy, there's a story. Every year, our school hosts three bake sales—one in the fall to raise funds for the football team, another in the winter for basketball, and the last in the spring for – surprise, surprise – baseball. My mom as one of the senior members of the Booster Club participates in every single one of them.

Never mind that her daughter has shown exactly zero inclination to support any sports teams ever. My mother insists on donating baked goods. Homemade, of course. Once, I suggested the booster club host a bake sale to buy new sound equipment for the drama club, because the feedback on their mics was horrendous, and I swear, my mom just about killed herself encouraging me to get involved. "Oh Danielle, I had no idea you were into theater!" and "Tell me when I'll get to see you in a play."

Never, Mom. Never.

Then, I had to go and break her heart by telling her that the only reason I'd mentioned it was because the whole school has to sit through the musical every year and the screeching was giving me a headache.

Anyway, last Saturday, I woke up to a kitchen filled, quite literally, with cupcakes. Every single surface covered in cupcakes. Everyone else's mom just swings by Food Lion and buys a pie or some cookies, but my mom has to do everything from scratch. Kill me now.

Almost as soon as I walked in the kitchen, she began hounding me to help her frost them. She pointed to a bag sitting on the counter with one of those little plastic tips that makes the icing look all swirly and professional.

Then she waved the freshly baked pan of cupcakes under my nose. "Red velvet. Don't they smell amazing?"

I rolled my eyes. "Positively divine."

This was, of course, before the whole stolen car fiasco. I ended up spending the whole of my Saturday morning squirting buttercream icing on about a hundred cupcakes that my classmates are going to just shove in their mouths and forget about in two seconds flat. Through the whole thing, my mom hovered over my shoulder and made annoying comments like:

"Try for a better swirl on the next one."

"Oh, that one has too much icing."

Eventually, I lost my cool and threw the bag of icing down and told her to just do it herself since I can't do anything right.

I was so annoyed that in Homeroom on Monday, when Mr. Craig asked about our weekends, I spilled the whole story. Even though my go-to defense mechanism in school is to speak only when teachers force you to.

Now Mr. Craig wants to know whether I've "resolved" the situation with my mom. I don't know. Does hiding a massive secret about being pregnant count as "resolving?"

Probably not.

I shrug my shoulders. "I think she's gotten over it. I mean," I glance around the room. "The cupcakes were a hit. They sold every last one of them, so what's the big deal?"

Mr. Craig leans forward on his knees. "Why do you think it was so important for your mom that you help make them?"

"Because she's a control freak and when I'm slaving away in the kitchen with her, it gives her an opportunity to boss someone around?"

Mr. Craig cocks his head. "I don't think that's it."

The obvious answer is that she "wants to spend time with me" or something like that, but I'm not in the mood.

* * *

"Danielle," Mr. Craig's voice stops me before I have a chance to escape to the hallway. "Can you stay back a second?"

I turn slowly, letting my classmates leave the room. "Yeah?"

He pulls my Creative Writing journal out of the milk crate by the window. "I was wondering if we could talk about your writing assignment."

He means the poem I wrote on Tuesday. I give what I hope is a noncommittal shrug. "The assignment was secrets, right? I wrote a poem about having a secret."

Mr. Craig nods and flips open the notebook to the page, then reads the poem aloud while my cheeks burn with embarrassment. When he's finished, he looks straight at me. "What do you mean by 'all will see what your secret has done to you?'" he asks.

I shake my head. "It doesn't mean anything."

"Does it have anything to do with why you left school last Thursday?"

God, I hope he can't read minds. "No."

He sits on the edge of the desk closest to me, in that way teachers do when they want to relate to you. Like, look how cool I am, I'm a teacher who sits on desks. Eyeroll.

"Everyone was really worried about you, you know. And if there's something that happened to you, that you don't feel like you can talk about," he pauses, looks me dead in the eye, "just know that your teachers—everyone here—we care about you. We're here to listen and to help."

Oh my God, my eyes go wide. He thinks I'm being abused or something.

"I promise, I'm fine," I say. "Nothing bad is happening here. Just normal teenage angsty stuff."

"Glad to hear it."

As soon as he hands me a pass to my next class, I bolt out of there.

Last Quarter

Over the next few days, Mom treats me like a princess. Almost to the point that I suspect she knows. On Monday, she makes eggs for breakfast. Just about the worst possible choice. The second I see them, my stomach roils. They smell of butter, and I can see the flecks of pepper on their yolks. Mom can do sunny-side up like a short-order cook at a diner. They're restaurant quality. But I know if I take a bite, I'm going to empty my stomach all over the place.

"Maybe I'll just have toast," I suggest timidly, and her head snaps up.

"I wish I had known that before I started cooking." Is that disappointment I hear? Of course it is.

"I'm sorry." I reach across the island and grab a piece of toast off the plate in the center and bite into it. No butter. No jam. Just plain whole wheat bread. For some reason, it's heavenly.

She eyes me for a few seconds then puts the spatula down and walks around the island in our kitchen to where I'm sitting on the stool. Then, she presses her hand to my forehead.

"Not feverish. You look a little green."

Dammit, she knows.

But I play it off with a shrug. "I think I ate some bad sushi with Jeremiah last night."

That gets her sympathy. "Do you want to stay home from school today?"

Uh oh. Dangerous territory. She hardly ever lets me stay home. She's one of those "education is important" moms who would send me to school with walking pneumonia if she thinks I can handle it. If I take her up on this offer, she's going to investigate. Try to figure out what's *really* wrong with me.

Plus, all the pregnancy research I've been doing on my phone–incognito search for the win–says morning sickness can last for weeks. No way she'll let me miss school every time I puke.

I shake my head. "No. I'm fine." I slide off the stool and head back toward the stairs. "I'll let you know."

I can feel her eyes on me the entire time, so I have to wait until I'm out of her line of sight before I race for the bathroom, falling to my knees just in time.

Toast didn't work out so great for me after all. Maybe I'll just start skipping breakfast. I know it's the most important meal of the day and all, but I don't think that counts when you're just upending it into the toilet five minutes later.

New Moon

Jeremiah has a Taekwodo tournament on Saturday, which gives me the perfect excuse to avoid my mom. Nothing I've ever done has disappointed her as much as this pregnancy will. I want to hold on to whatever love she might have left before I lose it forever.

Harder with Jeremiah. I can't miss his tournament. I haven't missed a tournament since we became official. I'm a very supportive girlfriend. Though keeping a secret likes this feels like the exact opposite of supportive. It feels like cheating.

I sit on the bleachers behind his family—he's got a huge family, and there's not enough room on the row for me—and try to focus on his forms, but all I can think about is my secret pregnancy. He does three of them—two without weapons, then another with his weapon of choice. He almost always uses a sword, and he's really good. Scary good. Sometimes I think about him defending my honor or something, like a knight. Someone insults me, and he just whips out that sword. Except the one he practices with isn't sharp, of course. But it's still pretty wild seeing him move, all fast and strong. Unfortunately for me, I'm all out of honor.

Normally, I could watch him all day. But today, all I can think about is this secret. I know I have to tell him. I keep trying, but every time I get close, the secret feels so big and impossible, and my heart starts racing, and I open my mouth to say something, then before I can get a word out, he's already started talking about something else.

And it feels rude to interrupt him.

It's been almost three weeks, and I'm not stupid. Pretty soon, I won't have a choice. Pretty soon the whole school will know.

All I can think about is this secret. I don't even see his sword forms, I'm too busy staring off into space, thinking about the secret and feeling terrible.

I hate this feeling, the I-messed-up feeling, and I've got it all to myself.

When Jer's mom turns around and asks me about school, I almost blurt it out. "I'm pregnant!" but I don't. I hide it back inside, buried in the depths of my stomach where only I know about it.

Instead, I force a smile. "It's okay, I guess."

"Are you taking any good classes this year?" She's got this smile on her face, and I think she's finally forgiven me for stealing Jer's car which makes me feel a thousand times worse about what I'm really keeping from her.

"Creative Writing, with Mr. Craig," I mumble. I hate to admit it, but as wacky as Mr. Craig is, it's still my favorite class.

"Oh, that's right." She turns all the way around to look at me and places a hand on my knee. "Jeremiah said you like to write poetry."

I can feel my cheeks getting hot. It was hard enough opening up enough to let Jer read my poetry. I didn't realize he was going to tell his mom about it.

I shake my head. "It's no good."

"I'm sure that's not true."

Thankfully, the last competitor finishes his forms, and it's time for the judges to calculate scores. Jeremiah saunters back over to his family, still in his uniform, the black belt tied snug around his waist. His parents immediately engulf him in hugs and forget about me.

Good.

When he catches my eye, I smile. He crinkles his eyebrows, like he can tell something is up, but before he can reach me, I duck out with some excuse about needing to use the bathroom. Perched on top of a toilet, I can think, or at least pretend to think. Try to think. Fail miserably at thinking.

Tell him, my inner voice screams. *TELL HIM!* I know I should. It shouldn't be this hard. I should be able to just blurt it out.

And then what? Will he still love me when he finds out? Everyone knows how this story goes. Girl gets pregnant, guy can't get away fast enough.

Am I so horrible for wanting to hold on to him as long as possible?

Jeremiah's not like that. He is good and kind, and he loves me. That will be enough.

* * *

I meet him where he waits by his car, his bag of equipment already stowed in the back. As soon as he sees me, his eyes light up, and within seconds, I am buried in his chest, savoring the warmth and comfort of those strong arms. Even the faint smell of sweat along his collarbone. It is enticing.

His fingers run through my hair. "You okay?"

I nod wordlessly and glance at him. How could I ever think he would desert me? When he clearly loves me?

I reach up and wrap my arms around his neck, leaning forward to press my lips into his. His lips are warm and soft. Safe. He responds immediately, pulling me closer. We haven't been this close in so long, I haven't realized how much I missed it. The two of us. I deepen the kiss.

My mind goes blank. All the worry of the past weeks, all the guilt of hiding this secret, gone. Now, it is just Jeremiah and his body pressed against mine, and the warmth building in my lower stomach. When he breaks away, I suck in a breath, dizzy from endorphins pumping through my veins.

He chuckles, his jaw brushing my cheek. "Let's get out of here."

"Yeah," I gasp. "Yeah, definitely."

After all, the damage has already been done.

Waxing Gibbous

Every time I open my mouth to tell Jeremiah, the words won't come out. In the end, I write it in a note. The worry, of course, is that someone else might find it and read it, so I have to make sure I hand it to him directly. No sliding it in his locker like I used to when we first starting dating. Unimportant little secrets. This one's a bit bigger.

I have to make sure only he reads it. And I have to make sure we're alone. Because I'm not sure how he'll react.

I mean, Jer has never ever gotten angry. Like, never in his life. Not that I've seen at least. I think it's because he has so many siblings. He learned how to stifle the anger emotion early, since there was always something to fight about. The guy quotes Yoda, and not ironically. He just really buys into that whole Zen-master thinking. It's the taekwondo that does it. It gives him a mellow other guys don't have. Another reason I love him so much.

It also gives him the ability to break a piece of wood with a single punch. I've seen him do it. I'm not scared of him, but this is pretty hefty news I'm slinging at him.

I wouldn't put it past him to handle it badly. Hell, I sure did.

I spend the entire day writing and rewriting the note. It's kind of funny, because I can lay down poetry so easily, and it just seems to flow, but a few simple sentences… not so much. At first, I start with a lengthy explanation of how much I love him and all the gushy gross boyfriend/girlfriend stuff. But I end up scrapping it because Jer knows I'm not an ooey-gooey girl. Actually, I kind of hate that sort of stuff.

So, then I write a big long explanation of how I got into this particular mess, but I mean… he was there. He should know.

Eventually I decide to keep it simple:

Dear Jeremiah,
I'm pregnant.
Love Dani

That should do the trick.

On Thursdays, he helps teach taekwondo to little kids at the studio, which my mom adores because it, "looks so good on a college application." Normally, he comes by my house afterward to study or watch TV or something, but today, I offer to ride with him.

"Really?" he asks.

I shrug. "Am I crazy for wanting to hang out with you?"

"I'm just going to be walking around telling little kids to sit still."

"I know." I grip his fingers. "I don't care."

For thirty minutes, I sit on the bleachers and watch Jeremiah with the kids. I spend the time folding and unfolding the paper about a million times until the initial crease has been lost among the crumples. I unfold, I refold, and I consider pitching it. But then I would have to actually say the words out loud, and the thought of that makes me want to puke.

When the class is over, he slides his shoes back on and walks over to me. "Ready to go?"

I nod. I can't form words right now. I can barely see his face.

The studio is filled with over-eager mothers and excited children. During class changes, the place is packed and uncomfortable. This is the absolute worst place to talk to Jeremiah, so I stuff the note into my pocket and follow him to his car.

"You want anything to eat?" he asks while we're walking. He pauses at the passenger side door and opens it for me. His little acts of chivalry make my insides burn with guilt.

"No thanks."

"You haven't really been eating much the past couple of weeks."

He's noticed. I knew someone would. Lunch has been torture. I can't handle the greasy school food. Even just looking at it makes me feel nauseous.

"I'm sure my mom's made something," I say. "We can just head to my house."

"Okay."

While he drives, I twirl the ring dangling from my necklace. The ring he gave me for my sixteenth birthday. A gold band with my birthstone cut in the shape of a heart. I know he loves me, but this is so hard.

He parks the car on the street in front of my house and starts to open the door.

"Wait," I force out. "I… uh…"

Jer drops his hand and slumps back into his seat. "Is something wrong?"

I take a deep breath for courage, then push the note into his hands.

"What's this?"

"Just read it," I mumble.

He nods. "Okay."

Jer unfolds the paper, and I force myself to watch. It would be cowardly to look away, and I hate cowards. I stare the entire time. Even though it takes Jer forever, like time slowed to a stop or something. He drags out every second of the unfolding process. Maybe I shouldn't have wadded it up so much.

Finally, it's open, and he reads the single sentence. I glue my eyes to his face, searching for any sign that he's upset.

At first, he just gapes at the paper in his hands, and the car is silent. Deadly silent.

Then, he looks up at me. "Is this a joke?"

I make an awkward choking noise. "I wish."

"You'd tell me, right? You have kind of a sick sense of humor."

I do, but does he have to remind me at this exact moment?

"No, Jer," I whisper. "Not a joke."

"But…" he stammers, looking back at the paper. "How?"

"I think the general consensus is that it occurs when two people have unprotected sex."

He frowns. "Very funny, Dani. We only did it like three times!"

"Yeah, well… it only takes once."

"Stop joking around," he snaps, "this is serious."

"I know."

"How long have you known?" he demands.

Gulp. The question I've been dreading, but I have to be honest. If I want any hope of salvaging things with Jer, I have to be honest.

"Four weeks."

His mouth falls open.

"Since…"

"Since you stole my car," he finishes for me. It's like everything clicks into place. "Where did you go?"

"To the beach where we…"

He slumps over his steering wheel, hiding his face in his arms. "Jesus Christ, Dani."

"I'm sorry."

"What were you thinking?"

"I don't know." I reach out to touch him but he pulls away. "I was just scared, and I didn't know how to tell you, and…" I'm still so scared. I just can't get the words out.

My voice trails off, and for a moment, we're both sitting there, alone in his car. In silence. Jeremiah won't look at me. It feels like the temperature has dropped ten degrees and I wrap my arms around myself. I haven't felt cold in weeks—hormonal hot flashes are real. Turns out, I just needed to massively disappoint my boyfriend to feel cold again.

"I'm sorry," I whisper again, turning away to stare at my front lawn, immaculately kept up of course. My mom, as an HOA representative, not only maintains the HOA rules, she exceeds them. Our lawn looks like it could be on the cover of *Better Homes and Gardens.*

After a while, he lifts his head, but he still won't look at me. Instead, he fixes his gaze on the street lamp in front of us. "What are you going to do about it?"

The coolness in his voice brings tears to my eyes, but I absolutely will not let them escape. I hate crying. Crying solves nothing. The unspoken A-word hangs between us. That should be enough to send me reeling, but it's the "you" that kills me. No more "we." No more "us." This is my problem, and mine alone.

"I don't know."

"Have you told your mom?"

My voice shakes. "Not yet."

Finally, he looks at me, and that's enough to send the tears flowing.

"I'm really scared, Jer."

His face softens, and he leans across the arm rest to hug me. His broad shoulders provide the best comfort in the world.

"I don't know what to do," I whimper.

He squeezes my shoulders. "We'll figure it out."

We… Thank God. I'd die if I didn't have Jer. He's the only good thing I have going for me these days. He waits while I cry myself out. Apparently, I've been saving up tears for weeks, because I sob for a long time, and when I pull away, he's got a disgusting mess of snot and tears on the shoulder of his T-shirt.

I wipe my face with the sleeve of my hoodie. Super sexy. If only I had been this gross ten weeks ago, then I never would have gotten into this mess.

When I've made my splotchy, disgusting face as presentable as I can, I lock eyes with him. His face is blank, emotionless. That's the problem with all the Zen-Yoda martial arts training. He's downright impossible to read sometimes.

"Are you mad at me?" I ask.

He opens his mouth, pauses, then shakes his head. "No."

Except… that pause kind of makes me think he is.

He decides not to come inside for dinner. A relief, really, because the way he looks at me now, there's no way he'd be able to face my mom. I don't even know if I am. My mom makes everything big, too big, and my problem already feels astronomical.

When I walk in the door, still looking like a mess, she jumps up from the sofa. "Dani! Have you been crying?"

Well, obviously, but I lie. "No."

"Your face is all red and puffy."

"I'm fine, Mom."

She follows me up the stairs to my room. "Is something wrong? Dani, talk to me."

"Nothing's wrong, Mom." We're in an awful race, me trying to get away, her trying to catch me, and I'm losing.

"Did you and Jeremiah have a fight?"

I don't know. Did we? "No," I say, "it's just allergies."

Mom pulls ahead of me and forces me to look at her. "Don't lie to me."

"Can we just drop it?"

"I want to know what's wrong," she insists. She leans on my door frame, preventing my escape into Dani-zone.

"I swear, I'm fine Mom."

"You've been so emotional lately."

You would be too, if you were sixteen and just found out you were pregnant, I think wryly. "Okay," I say, "I'll do my best not to be emotional anymore. Happy?"

She narrows her eyes. "No. That doesn't make me happy. I want to know what's going on."

She's not backing down, so I give her what she wants. "Yes," I say with exasperation, "Jer and I fought. Okay? We're fine, we just had a little argument. It's not that big of a deal."

Mom purses her lips like she's not sure she believes me. "Sometimes, I think you and Jeremiah are too serious. You're just a child. You shouldn't be pinning all your hopes and dreams on one boy."

I scoff. Or you know, my entire life.

Lucky me, her watch beeps at that precise moment. She looks down at it. "I have a Booster Club meeting." She sighs and looks at me. "This conversation isn't over, okay? But I have to run."

"Fine, whatever." Maybe I'll be asleep before she gets home, so she doesn't think pester me to talk more. At the very least, I can pretend.

She nods. "Okay. Love you. See you tonight." She pauses at my doorway, still watching me, and I groan.

"Love you too, Mom."

She'll keep hounding me until she hears it. Better to just get it out.

Waxing Gibbous

The next few days are some of the worst of my life. Jeremiah says he wants to support me, but he gets this look in his eyes every time we're together, like his dreams are being crushed before they ever had a chance to start flying. It's enough to drive me insane. We walk in the school hallways between classes, and at first, everything seems the same. He carries my books for me, just like normal. He still opens doors for me, my sweet, caring boyfriend.

But now he's silent, and every once in a while, he lets out a gigantic sigh. Like hope is lost.

I get it. I do. I was the same way. He noticed. Now, we're in it together, and I feel better, honestly, knowing that Jeremiah and I are a team again. But he clearly feels worse. I think he wishes I had just taken care of it without him. Ignorance really is bliss, and I stole that away from him.

Finally, I confront him about the A-word. "I think I should probably visit a clinic, you know…" I gesture at my stomach, "for this."

He looks down at where I'm pointing, and for a second, his eyes go distant, and I'm not sure he is even aware of what I'm talking about. Then he shakes his head. "So you've made a decision? You're going to get rid of it?"

"I'm not sure, but I figure I should probably at least keep the option open…" I glance around the hallway. "Right?"

"Yeah."

I take a deep breath. "Um… can you drive me?"

He nods. "Yeah."

"I was thinking after school next Monday? My mom has to work late. Some quarterly review thing."

"Okay."

He's not even looking at me. His face is turned toward me, but his eyes drift and his mind is elsewhere.

"Okay," I say. I lean up on my toes and kiss his cheek. "I love you."

"Love you too," but his voice is distant. Some of the magic is lost.

* * *

I catch up to Shelby in the hallway after school, grabbing her arm as she passes. "Hey, can we talk?"

She sighs dramatically. "Yeah? What's up?"

I take a deep breath. "Um, so this is kind of hard."

"Can you make it quick? I'm running late."

I hate being rushed, and it's not like this is the sort of news one can just drop on a person without a real discussion. Already, she's turning to leave, more anxious to spend time with Miles than to hear what I have to say.

She rolls her eyes. "Dani, c'mon." She starts walking away. "Stop wasting my time."

She makes it half a step, but I grab her arm. "I'm pregnant."

That gets a reaction. She stops dead in her tracks and turns around slowly. "What?"

"I'm pregnant. Jer and me… I just thought you should know."

"Whoa!" she says, her eyes travelling straight to my stomach. "When did you find out?"

"A while ago."

"Have you told Jeremiah yet?"

I nod. Her face is hard to read. If I didn't know any better, I'd think she was happy, or something.

"You can't tell anyone," I say, stupidly.

She shrugs. "I won't."

"Promise, Shelby!"

"I promise. Geez! I won't tell. Stop being such a drama queen."

She stares at me for a few seconds, like she expects me to say something else. But what else is there to say? After this bombshell, I'm pretty much tapped out on big revelations. With a nod, she turns and leaves me standing alone in the deserted hallway.

* * *

The next day, Shelby breaks off laughing when I walk into Homeroom. She gives me a look, almost chagrined, then sinks back into her seat. I meander through the desks until I sit in the one next to hers. "What's so funny?"

"Nothing."

The girls behind her snicker and avoid my eyes.

I frown. "Were you talking about me?"

"You're so paranoid, Dani."

But, I don't feel paranoid. I feel completely justified. Because the girls are still laughing under their breath, and when I glance over at them, they learn toward each other and whisper something to each other.

I lean toward Shelby. "Did you tell them?"

"Tell them what?"

I gape. She knows exactly what. "About my situation."

She smirks and her eyes dart to the pair behind me. "Dani, seriously. I promised I wouldn't tell, didn't I?"

I guess I don't look convinced, because she leans over my desk. "You just need to take your mind off things. Come over to my house tonight. We can take it easy, movies and junk food. Girls night."

"I don't think a chick flick is going to magically fix this for me, Shelby." Not to mention the mere idea of grease and salt makes me feel sick.

She purses her lips and slinks back into her chair. "Suit yourself."

* * *

"Over the next few weeks," Mr. Craig says as he drops our composition notebooks onto our desks, "we will be exploring the theme of *Loneliness*."

Creative Writing is great. We literally get to write whatever we want, so long as we're addressing the theme. And we have these crazy prompts every morning. Things like: You wake up in the middle of the 19th century. What happens next?

"Everyone," Mr. Craig continues, "has dealt with loneliness. It's as universal as love and hate, jealousy… pain. Loneliness is part of the human condition. We are social creatures by nature, so what do we do when our social circle starts to break down?"

He stops at my desk and hands me my notebook, looking me square in the eye. "Even those of us who think they don't need anyone feel the pang of loneliness from time to time." He walks away. "Ten minutes of free write. Tap into that feeling. When was the last time you felt utterly alone? Describe every minute detail of it."

He stops at the front of the classroom and puts his hands on his hips. "And… Go."

Oh boy. I could write a whole freaking novel.

Waning Gibbous

True to his word, Jeremiah drives me to the clinic after school on Monday. The waiting room looks exactly like you'd expect it to—off-white walls, dingy blue chairs. Everyone sitting around avoiding each other's eyes. It smells like shame. I glance down at my stomach. How many of the girls in the room are here for the same reason I am? Got themselves into a bit of trouble? Need a quick fix.

At least Jer loves me, I think, then I stop myself. It's pretty crummy to come to a women's health clinic and start judging the other girls there. Granny would be ashamed. She's all about the sisterhood. That bond between women. She used to say things like, "when one woman suffers, we all suffer."

I can believe it. I look around the room. Every one of us looks the same. Nervous and scared. We suffer together.

This is the only place in a twenty-five-mile radius that'll perform an abortion, and after several lengthy conversations with Jeremiah, during which he reminded me multiple times that he was applying to MIT, we ultimately decided this was the best choice.

He keeps saying he doesn't want to pressure me into it. "It's your..." he pauses, and I get the feeling he wants to say "problem" but knows he shouldn't. "Body," he finishes.

It really is the best choice. It makes sense. If we don't get rid of it, then all our plans will be derailed. And there's time enough for children when we're married. After college.

So why do I feel so horrible?

Jeremiah doesn't seem to be feeling it. Instead, he sits next to me, playing on his phone, seemingly oblivious to the plight of the women in the room. I count myself lucky, because I have someone with me. Some of the girls here are alone or with a friend or family member, and they all look scared. It makes me wonder if they can read the terror on my own face.

I start to wonder about their stories. How did they end up sitting in the same waiting room as me? Contemplating the same choice?

I reach across the armrest and grip Jeremiah's free hand. He gives it a half-hearted squeeze, then loosens his hold and returns to his game.

My body, my problem. I am just as alone as the other women here.

I can't help but feel disappointed in Jeremiah's utter lack of concern. He's seemingly divorced himself from the situation, as if he thinks that it's already been solved. No more need to worry. But I'm worried. I spent the last week researching abortion stories online, and of course the Internet was filled with everything that could go wrong. With pictures. Not a smart choice.

"Danielle?" A sharp voice startles me out of my thoughts. "Danielle?"

I stand and the rush of movement makes my stomach flop. The nausea. I won't miss that. Luckily, the moment passes, and I follow the nurse through the wooden door and down a short hall. Jeremiah stays in the waiting room, eyes glued to his phone screen. I wonder if he even realizes I've left his side.

"Full name?" the nurse asks, bored.

"Danielle Miller."

"Date of birth?"

"April 16, 2003."

She glances at her clipboard with tight judgmental lips. "Step on the scale."

I do and she jots down a number. "What was your pre-pregnancy weight?"

"About 145, I think."

Another note on the paper, then she points to the bathroom. "Leave a sample on the tray."

"A sample?" I ask.

"Urine."

I'm so stupid. I should have known. I went pee right before we left school, and now it feels like I've gone completely dry. Still the nurse likes one of those take-no-excuses types, so I do what she says, which means sitting on the toilet for an eternity before managing to squeeze out the bare minimum.

I leave the bathroom and follow the nurse into an exam room. She is all business, going through a dozen routine measurements—blood pressure, temperature, pulse—all while telling me to put on the gown and asking embarrassing questions.

"How long have you been sexually active?"

"Like three months."

"Date of your last period?"

I have no idea. Not really. I try to tell her that I've always been irregular, but she just wants an answer. I end up guessing, giving her a date toward the beginning of August. Sounds about right.

She frowns then lifts the phone off the wall behind her. "We need an ultrasound." When she hangs up, she looks me right in the eye.

I hunch my shoulders. "Why do I have to get an ultrasound if I'm just going to get rid of it?"

"We need to see how far along you are."

She walks me down the hall to a dark room where the ultrasound technician is already seated at her computer, typing away. Another person who barely acknowledges my presence as I walk in, and instead talks to the chart in her hand. "Danielle Miller?"

"Yeah."

"Have a seat."

I do as she asks, while she continues to type away. Eventually, she flips on the machine. "You'll need to lift your shirt and unbutton your jeans."

I nod, following the instructions. Sweet release. Those jeans have been feeling a little too tight lately.

She uses a white towel to push the front of my pants lower, revealing my bare belly onto which she squirts a dollop of cold gel without any warning, followed immediately by the sensor. She angles it around, searching for something in the grainy black and white shadows on her computer screen. Then, she stops.

"Heartbeat 132 per minute," she mutters, then types into her computer.

I watch her in silence as she pauses again and taps a few buttons on her keyboard.

"Measuring 42 millimeters," she pauses, types, "which puts us at about eleven weeks gestation."

"What's that mean?" I ask.

She doesn't answer. Maybe she can't, since she's not a nurse.

Instead she looks at me for the first time since I walked in. "Do you want to see it?"

"Um…" I'm not sure. Do I? Maybe a little.

"No pressure," she adds. "Some women want to. Others prefer not."

I stare into her eyes. Plain brown and hidden behind the geekiest pair of thick plastic rims I have ever seen. But they're kind eyes, like she's been doing this a while, and she gets it. I get the feeling she understands, so I nod. "Sure, I guess."

She turns the screen around, and there it is. My big mistake. I've never really seen an ultrasound before, except on TV shows. This is completely different. I'm shocked at how human it looks already. Not completely, but I can tell it has a head. And I can see its heart beating, little rhythmic flutters in an expanse of grainy grays.

My heart races along with its, and I start to feel dizzy, so I look away. "Okay, I'm good. Thanks."

She nods and pulls the screen back toward her. She back to her job, now. A sheet of pictures prints below her desk, and she slides it into my chart, then buzzes the nurse to take me back to the room.

Once back in the exam room, I'm told the doctor will be "right with you" which it turns out is code for "you'll be waiting for half an hour."

Half an hour I spend thinking about the little fluttering heartbeat on the ultrasound screen. It was so real. Not like a pair of pink lines on a urine stick at all. But like a real human.

I wait so long that I start to wonder how Jeremiah is doing in the front lobby. Apparently, he's thinking the same thing because he texts me to ask how much longer it'll be.

"Not sure," I reply, "Doc hasn't been in yet."

The three dots appear at the bottom of the screen, meaning he's typing a response, but they disappear and reappear two times before he finally sends something.

"K."

I sigh. What a letdown.

The doctor, it seems, is a fifty-something year old balding man with a belly farther out than his nose. Like everyone else in the clinic, he looks at my chart more than he looks at me.

"Good afternoon, Daisy," he says.

"Dani," I correct him.

He nods and flips through my paperwork. "Eleven weeks along… Date of birth… hmm…" his eyebrows raise. "Sixteen?" he asks, looking at me for the first time.

"Yeah."

"Do your parents know you're here?"

"No." Suddenly, I'm freaking out. Do they need to? What if I need them to sign off on this procedure? I had hoped to avoid telling them altogether.

"Well," he settles onto a stool and tosses the chart on the counter before snapping on a pair of gloves, "let's see what we have going on. Are you allergic to latex?"

"I don't know." The best way to find out is to use a condom, and I kind of skipped that step. Oops.

He instructs me to scoot my bottom to the end of the table and let my legs fall open. "Have you ever had a pelvic exam before?" he asks.

"Um… no."

"So, we'll need a pap smear."

Within seconds, the nurse has a gigantic Q-tip ready along with a terrifying looking metal contraption. I'm struck with the sense that everything is happening fast. Too fast, like I can't escape. My heart pounds in my ears.

"You'll feel some pressure," he says about half a second before sticking that metal thing in my you-know-where. Then I get the delightful sensation of the Q-tip scraping my insides. I glare at the ceiling and try not to think about how this gross old guy is prodding around in my vagina while Jeremiah sits in the waiting room playing on his phone. It just feels so unfair.

As soon as he's done, he yanks the stuff out of me, pulls his gloves off, and stands.

I release the breath that I was holding the entire time.

He launches right into his speech. "You're too far along to be able to have a medical abortion. Next time, try to come in as soon as you know you're pregnant." No point in telling him that I'm praying that there never is a "next time."

"For now," he continues, "Go home and discuss your options with your parents. You're under eighteen, so we can't do anything surgical without their permission. It's easier if you get the procedure done before thirteen weeks, but that doesn't give you a lot of time to decide. After that, it's more expensive and a harder recovery."

"How much will it cost?"

He never looks up from the chart. "The nurse can walk you through the details." It's a comfort he doesn't know her name either. He hands the chart to her, opens the door, and walks out. I've never felt so dirty in my life.

Turns out I'm looking at about 450 bucks to get the abortion. That is, if I get it in the next two weeks. After that, it goes up to 600. I sigh. I don't have the kind of money. Jeremiah might have something saved from work, but I'm not sure how much. And can he afford to spend it on this when he's trying to go to college next year? Even if I could get the procedure without my parents knowing, I would still need their help to pay for it.

Once she's answered all my questions, the nurse steps out as well. "Get dressed, then you can leave. Have a good day."

There is nothing good about this day.

I stop by the desk on my way to the waiting room to pay the thirty-dollar fee for being seen in the clinic. The receptionist hands me a business card. "You'll need to call to set up the next appointment."

I nod, the push through the door.

The waiting room has cleared quite a bit. Only a few people are scattered across the room. Jeremiah is seated in the exact same spot, still staring at his phone screen. I walk over to him. "Ready to go?"

He looks up. "Yeah. You good?"

Nowhere near good, but I hate for him to see me cry. "Yeah, I guess."

I follow a step behind him out the door. The air is turning cool, and it smells like fall. Halloween is in two days, but I haven't spent a second thinking about it. I'm already scared enough. I don't need monsters, I have my reality.

The leaves have all turned red and orange. Usually, I love the colors of fall. I could spend hours watching the wind rustle through the branches, the way the leaves dance their way to the ground. Not this year. This year, I can only think about myself.

Jeremiah is silent on the drive home. I spend the time with my face pressed against the glass, watching the sky turn dark. We are strangers trapped in this car together. He parks his car in my driveway but makes no move to get out.

I keep my eyes on the dashboard. The little green numbers on the clock read 5:24. "Do you want to come in?"

"I have a lot of homework." His voice is empty.

"You could work on it at my house," I suggest hopefully.

"I think I'll just go home."

I glance at him, but his face is stoic. "I guess I'll see you tomorrow," I say.

"I guess so."

I pull the door handle and climb out, then trudge my way up the sidewalk, past the Halloween decorations my mom insists on putting out every year, to my front door. Only after I shut the door behind me do I realize that Jeremiah and I parted without saying "I love you."

We haven't done that in months.

Third Quarter

I don't even know. Do I do it? Do I not? I need someone other than Jeremiah to talk to about this. He clearly wants me to. He might not be saying it, but I can tell.

Mom still hasn't figured it out. Or if she has, she's not saying anything. Which means I'm all alone. Perfect for Mr. Craig's writing prompts, but not so perfect for me.

The time you felt most alone.

Right now.

A time when you've felt alone in the middle of a crowd.

Right now.

What is the largest contributor to human loneliness?

I write a poem for that:

> *The loneliness of a choice made wrong*
> *Cleaving a bond once thought strong*
> *Two souls connected*
> *Now fall apart*
> *Lost in the rhythm of a third beating heart*
> *A single choice could save what was lost*
> *But at what cost?*
> *Yes, at what cost?*

Mr. Craig keeps me after class again. I'm getting so sick of our little meetings. "Is there something you want to talk about, Danielle?"

"No."

"You've been withdrawn lately."

Just lately? I've always been withdrawn. But I see what he means.

"I'm fine. Just dealing with stuff."

"Boy trouble?"

Of the worst kind. "No."

He folds his arms. "Okay. Well, if you need to talk, you know where to find me."

Yeah, I think, *let me just chat with my forty-year-old male teacher about my grand abortion debate. No thank you.*

Then it hits me. There is one person I could talk to. The perfect person, because she won't even remember. Hell, she probably won't even know it's me.

I climb into Jeremiah's car at the end of the day. "I want to visit my Granny," I say.

His eyes dart to my face, then down to my stomach. "Why?"

"I just need someone to talk to."

"You can talk to me."

I pause. "Can I?"

He doesn't respond, but when we get to the cross-street, he turns. Jer's a good boyfriend.

"Do you want me to come in with you?" he asks. It's a nice gesture, but we both know he'd hate it. He's more uncomfortable around the elderly than I am. He's used to kids.

"No thanks," I point out the coffee shop across the street. "How about you go get us something to drink?"

"Aren't you supposed to lighten up on the caffeine?"

Oh yeah.

"Um, just get me a smoothie, I guess."

I find Granny in the rec room. She's knitting. Knitting is one of the few things she can still manage. She has a hard time concentrating on reading, but her fingers have the stitches memorized. Nurse Minnie says it's because it's muscle memory. Alzheimer's doesn't affect her muscles as much.

"Hey Granny," I say as I sit in the comfy chair next to her.

She looks up and smiles. "Oh Danielle, it's so good to see you."

"What are you making?"

"Oh, you know…" But I don't know. Maybe it's nothing, maybe she's just making a large expanse of fabric with no purpose other than to pass the time. It must be lonely, all these hours in the home.

"Um, I have something to tell you."

"Hmm?" She sets her knitting down.

"Um." Wow, it's still so hard to form the words. I really should practice in the mirror or something. I can just imagine Mom walking in while I'm practicing. Worst nightmare.

"Well, I guess I'm pregnant?" It comes out like a question. Sheesh, I should be beyond this.

The click-clack of her knitting needles stops. She looks me up and down, then smiles and reaches across the armrest to lay her hand on mine. "Oh, that's wonderful. Some good news, after losing Caleb."

Well, at least she thinks it's good news.

"Yeah," I agree. "But you know, Caleb died a long time ago."

"Did he?" She shakes her head confused. "But I remember the phone ringing all night long. Bert's mom on the other end. What's her name again?"

I think of the severe woman I've only met a handful of times. "Candace?"

"Yes, that's right." Granny concentrates on her knitting. "We flew out to Maine of course, the middle of winter, and we didn't even have the proper coats. But we had to see him. Our little boy, his lips had turned blue. So cold."

I don't know what to say. Mom's never told me anything about Caleb.

Granny's gaze meets mine. "But Hannah, you know you can't blame yourself forever. Even the police said it was only an accident."

My jaw drops. Police? An accident? And Mom blaming herself? This is the first time in weeks I've been able to think about anything other than my pregnancy.

"What happened?" I whisper, but Granny's mind has already turned to something else.

"The children from the church down the street are coming in two weeks."

I slump in my chair. "Oh."

Granny nods. "A Thanksgiving play. You should bring your baby."

"Right," I say, "Um, maybe."

We spend the rest of the time talking about nothing. Granny promises to knit the baby some clothes, but I know she'll forget. Maybe I should learn how to knit.

I can't shake what Granny told me about Mom and Caleb. I keep thinking about those first few years of my life. I was only a baby when Caleb died, but I remember this sense of Mom always hovering over me, but also holding herself at a distance. Maybe she didn't want to be close to me, after what happened with Caleb.

My whole life, I've felt like the wrong child had died. Because Mom clearly loved Caleb more than me. That much is obvious. Maybe she wishes it had been me.

I find Jeremiah standing outside the nursing home with a strawberry-kiwi smoothie in one hand and a hot green tea for himself in the other. Something must have shown on my face. The second he sees me, he rushes over, setting the drinks on the bench so he can grab my hands.

"Hey, are you okay?"

"Yeah," I mumble, "I just… I dunno."

"Did you tell your grandmother about…"

"Yeah."

"What did she say?"

I smile sadly. "That it's good news." I look up at him. "Is it?"

"I dunno."

I can't figure it out either. Sometimes I think of it as my big problem. Something that came into my life just to destroy it. But I love Jeremiah, and he loves me. I can't help but think that this baby, or fetus, or whatever is a real, tangible manifestation of that love.

And what would be bad about that?

I pick up the smoothie and take a sip. The cold, fruity liquid feels good sliding down my throat, coats my stomach, and takes an edge off the nausea that has been haunting me for weeks. Jeremiah pulls away and picks up his own drink. He's probably thinking it's too cold for a smoothie, but he doesn't have the hormonal hot flashes that I do. For a while, we're just standing there, sipping our drinks, together but not really together. I don't know what he's thinking about, but I can guess. The pregnancy, and the possibility of an abortion. My days are numbered. I need to decide soon.

As we walk back to his car, I break the silence. "Does your mom have a favorite child?"

Jer chokes on his tea. "What kind of question is that? Of course not!"

"Oh," I bite my lip. "I guess sometimes it feels like Mom loved Caleb more than me."

He pulls me to a stop, then traces my chin with his thumb. "Where is this coming from?"

I look up at him. "I'm not sure I can do it. It just feels wrong, you know? Mom lost a child, and it broke her. I can't imagine what it would do to her if I did the same thing. And I'd need her permission, and…"

He nods. "I get it."

"You sure?"

"Yeah," he says. "I kind of figured, actually."

"Really?"

"You're tenderhearted, Dani," he says, "no matter how much you pretend you're not. You're too sweet to ever hurt anything."

I bite my lip and mull his words around in my mind, trying to think of something to say. Anything that could make this easier, this decision I've made for the both of us.

But all I can think of is, "thanks."

Waxing Crescent

"We need to tell our parents." I lean against the locker next to Jeremiah's and watch him sort through his notebooks. "I mean, they're going to find out soon enough." We've been hiding it so long, I have no idea how they haven't. Last time I went bowling with my dad, I started to feel dizzy and had to sit out three frames.

Jer nods and shuts his locker, then tucks his books under one arm, and wraps the other around my shoulders. He squeezes. "Yeah, I've been thinking about that."

"And?"

"I think maybe we should just do it all at once, like peeling a Band-Aid off. Quick."

"And extra painful," I joke.

"Well," he says, "Like you said, we have to tell them eventually. Plus," he pauses and looks around. "If we're keeping it, then you'll need to go to the doctor. Like a real doctor."

Anyone other than that creep at the clinic. "Maybe we could do it this weekend?"

Jer shakes his head. "I can't. I have a Tae Kwon Do tournament in Raleigh. All day Saturday."

"Oh." He didn't tell me about it. I usually can't make the out-of-town ones anyway, but it would have been nice to be invited.

He clearly realizes the same thing, because he backtracks. "You want to ride with my parents and me?"

I shake my head. "No, it'll just be weird."

He breathes a sigh of relief. I get it. Lying is hard.

"Um," I say. "Maybe we could go out to eat somewhere on Wednesday? So we're not interfering with Thanksgiving."

"Both sets of parents?"

"And Ashley, too." Dad won't go anywhere without her.

Jeremiah nods. "Okay, let's do this."

* * *

Somehow, coming up with a plan to tell our parents actually makes it easier to face everyone else. I barely make it to homeroom on time, sliding into the seat behind Shelby just as the tardy bell rings. Mr. Craig nods at me, then goes back to taking attendance.

Shelby turns in her seat. "We need to talk."

"Why?"

She leans in closer, and I have to meet her in the middle just to hear what she has to say. "People are starting to wonder about you. They say you're getting fat. I've been hearing things."

So much for invisibility.

"I'm pregnant," I hiss, my lips less than an inch from her ear. "I'm not getting fat."

"I know," she replies, "But I can't exactly tell people that, can I? I don't know why you don't just get rid of it. It's what I would do."

Of course she would. Got a problem, just spend some money and fix it, then move on.

"It's too late," I whisper. "It's too expensive, and I'd need my mom's permission."

"Ladies!" Mr. Craig's voice interrupts whatever witty rejoinder Shelby had planned, making us both jump. "Something you'd like to share with the class?"

I feel like a caged animal, but Shelby raises a sarcastic eyebrow. "No."

"Great, then let's get started, shall we?"

We're discussing career paths today, but I can't pay attention. Now that I've decided to keep the baby, I know my options are limited. I could probably take online classes or go to night school if Mom watches the baby, but something tells me dorm rooms and frat parties aren't in my future anymore. It'll take me years to get a degree, and I can't exactly go to any school in the country. Driving distance only.

I spend the period doodling in my notebook until my eyelids slowly close. The next thing I feel is Mr. Craig shaking my shoulder.

"Danielle? Are you okay?"

"What?" I sit up and wipe drool from my mouth. "Where is everyone?"

"The bell rang," he explains, "class is over."

"Oh, sorry." I start to leave, but pause at the door, looking back at him. "Hey, Mr. Craig?"

"Yes?" He doesn't even look up, too busy getting ready for next class.

"I'm pregnant."

He stops moving and looks up slowly. "Do your parents know?"

I shake my head.

"Are you okay? Do you need help? Resources?"

Oh God, now I regret telling him. "You know, I gotta get to my next class," I say quickly, "Sorry, just forget it, okay?"

Then I dart out before he can hold me back any longer.

Full Moon

I'm a textbook procrastinator when it comes to dealing with tough situations. Which is how I almost forget to tell Mom about the dinner altogether. I texted Dad as soon as Jeremiah and I parted ways. But Mom? Oops, it slipped my mind. Or maybe I didn't want to face the music.

I don't have school on Wednesday, because of the Thanksgiving holiday, so I offer to go with Mom to work.

She nearly drops the waffle she was transferring onto my plate. "Really?"

"Is that okay?"

"Yes, of course. We'd love to have you come in."

I start smearing butter over the waffle, still hot from the iron. My appetite has come back with a vengeance, and Mom's noticed. She frowns as I pour syrup, then cut off a gigantic bite.

"Slow down, Dani."

"Sorry," I say through a mouthful of deliciousness. I swallow. "I'm just really hungry."

"Well, keep eating like that, and you'll put on a few pounds." She eyes my midsection. "Looks like you already have."

"Gee, thanks." Wait until she sees how much more weight I put on over the next few months. I watch her pour batter into the iron for her own waffle, significantly smaller than mine. She only fills up only a quarter of the iron, then, she leans on the counter next to me.

"Hey Mom?"

"Uh huh?" She picks up the newspaper. She's not really listening to me.

"Jer and I were thinking about having a big family dinner tonight, with all our parents."

She glares over the top of the newspaper. "Thanks for the warning."

"Sorry, I forgot."

"I hope I don't have to cook."

I shake my head. "No, we were thinking we could all go out to eat."

Mom purses her lips. She's thinking about Dad. Sure enough, "Will your father be there?"

"Yeah, he said he would."

"And Ashley?"

"He didn't say." I slide a bite of waffle through the pool of syrup on my plate. "I assume he's bringing her."

"Please tell me this isn't an engagement announcement. You're too young to be thinking about that."

"No, geez, Mom!" I scowl from across the kitchen island. "We're not getting married!" Yet.

Mom sighs. "Okay, fine."

Lucky for me, the waffle iron beeps and she gets up to get her food. I scarf down the rest of my own breakfast in record time, so I don't have to keep talking to her. Not that she wants to talk to me either.

I've already offered to go to work with her, so I'm kind of stuck on that end, but she's busy with some last-minute meetings trying to finalize plans before the break. "It's not Thanksgiving in Africa, you know." Which basically means, she thinks it's selfish of the charity to close for two days and give everyone a holiday. She'd be perfectly happy working her butt off for the children across the world, but she can barely stand to be around me.

I spend most of the day in the back room sorting through papers with her secretary. Joanie absolutely adores my mom, and she's not great at hiding it. But she also really likes me. Maybe Joanie's the sort of person who likes everyone.

We get along pretty well. Joanie plays music out of her cell phone, so I hardly notice the time flying by until my mom shows up in the doorway.

"Time to go, Dani, if we're going to make your dinner reservation."

I glance at my cellphone for the time. "Oh, wow. Okay." I grab my bag and sling it over my shoulder. "See ya, Joanie."

"Have a good weekend!" Yeah, Joanie is always happy.

We drive in silence to the restaurant. Jeremiah and his parents are already there. They greet my mom warmly, his mom plants a kiss on both of my mom's cheeks. She likes to think she's European or something. And his dad smiles broadly as he shakes her hand. "Good to see you again, Hannah. Especially under better circumstances." He glances my way, and I grit my teeth. Just wait and see, buster. The bomb I'm about to drop on you is a whole lot worse than a stolen car.

I catch Jer's eye, and he shrugs apologetically.

"Is Bert here yet?" Mom asks.

"Doesn't look like it," Jer says. He glances at the hostess. "We put our names in for a table already. I hope that's okay."

My mom—the queen of all things etiquette—nods. "Of course. Once two or more of the party has arrived, it's perfectly appropriate to be seated."

I roll my eyes. "If they call our names before Dad gets here, I can wait out front for them."

"Nonsense," Mom says, folding her arms. "He can figure it out." But the way she says it makes me think she wants Dad to be inconvenienced.

Sure enough, the hostess calls our party and we follow her to a large table in the back corner of the restaurant. As close to deserted as we can get, thank goodness. I can tell Mom's fuming because Dad is late. She's always going on about how irresponsible he is. I guess I can see her point. Dad likes his fun.

I make sure to sit next to Jeremiah. I'll need him for this. Mom sits on my other side, effectively making it impossible for Dad to sit next to me. But then, the only open spots at the long table are next to her, and across the table next to Jeremiah's mom. Which means Mom has to sit next to either Dad or Ashley. I don't know which one she'll hate more.

The waiter shows up to ask what we want to drink, and Dad still hasn't arrived. I can tell Mom's itching to comment on it, but he rolls in just in time to catch the waiter as he's leaving.

"A bottle of wine for the table. What do you want, Ashley? Cabernet?"

Ashley smiles and nods. I can smell the cigarette smoke on her from across the table.

Dad grins. "Hell, let's make it two." He hands the waiter his credit card. "On me. The whole meal."

"Bert..." my mom begins.

"Oh Hannah, don't tell me you've gone all dry in your old age. You used to be able to handle a bottle by yourself." He bustles around the table. "And that was on good days." Then he yanks me out of my chair, bumping Mom as he does and pulls me into a tight hug, planting a rough kiss on my cheek. "How's my beautiful girl?"

"Fine, Dad."

Every cell in my body screams to be left alone, so I can go back to being invisible between Jer and Mom, but Dad is an extrovert to the max. He's your classic middle management, Mr. Charisma, gets along with everyone and is the life of the party sort of guy. Sometimes I can't understand what my mom ever saw in him, because she's all business. She doesn't want to play, and all he ever does is play.

The waiter jots down Dad's wine order then heads back to the kitchen. Dad plops into the chair next to Mom and leans across her to talk to me. "I can get a glass for you, pumpkin. If you want."

"Bert!" Mom hisses. "She is sixteen." She punches every syllable.

He ignores her and waggles his eyebrows at me. I shake my head. "No thanks."

Then he looks at Jeremiah. "How 'bout you, kid?"

"No, sir." That's Tae Kwon Do training, right there. No breaking rules, but always be respectful to the adults.

I glance at Jeremiah, and I can tell he's thinking the same thing. Maybe this was a bad idea. I give his hand a squeeze beneath the table. We can handle this, if we do it together. He lays his hand on top of mine. Okay, here goes.

We agreed beforehand that we would wait until we were about halfway through dinner to tell everyone about the pregnancy. Mostly because we want everyone to be in a good mood, and partly because I figured my dad would order wine, and I figured maybe if everyone was a little inebriated, it would go better.

I was wrong.

Because we don't even get to the dinner. The drinks arrive, we place our food orders, then Mom turns in her seat—a literal ninety-degree turn—to look at me.

"Well," she says, "I think we're all wondering it. Why exactly are we having this meal together?"

Dad chuckles, but thankfully says nothing.

I take a deep breath. Every person at the table is looking at me, except Jeremiah who is staring at the wall above his dad's head. I guess this is on me.

"Um, well you see…" I look to Jeremiah for help.

"I thought we were waiting until after we ate to tell them."

"Tell us what?" Mr. Clark asks.

Mom pinches the bridge of her nose. "Spit it out, Danielle."

I keep talking. "Um, I guess… uh…" Oh God, it's just so hard.

"Dani's pregnant," Jeremiah blurts out. I wince.

For a second, the table is silent. None of Dad's inappropriate jokes. None of Mom's incessant nagging. Mr. and Mrs. Clark stare open-mouthed. Even Ashley knows to keep her mouth shut.

Then, they all start talking at once.

"How did this happen?"

"My God, what were you thinking?"

"How could you be so irresponsible?"

"You never think, Danielle!"

"Your futures will be ruined!"

"This is insanity."

"What are we going to do?"

Too much. I lay my head on the table and hide in my arms. Then, my dad slams his fist on the table, and everyone goes quiet. I chance a peek over my arms.

"There's an obvious solution here."

Everyone stares. I glance at Jeremiah who looks sick to his stomach.

"We'll just get rid of it," Dad says, and my heart stops.

"Bert!" Mom snaps.

Jeremiah glances at his parents, then stares at his lap. "We thought about that, but Da—I mean, we want to keep it."

Too late. Everyone knows he meant to say Dani. I am alone in this.

Mom looks at me with an expression I can't figure out, like she's not sure who I am. I look past her to my Dad.

"Dad, I…"

But he stands up before I can finish, shaking his head. "I have never been so disappointed in you." Mom stands up between us, so I can't see her face. But I can tell from her stance she's furious.

"But it was an accident!" I say, unable to hide the tears in my eyes.

"Yeah," Dad says as he tosses a wad of cash on the table to pay for the wine and grabs his coat, "we've had plenty of those, haven't we?"

"Stop it," Mom snaps.

Without another word, he pushes past Ashley toward the exit, and she scurries after him.

"I'm sorry," I whisper, even though he's too far away to hear.

Mom returns to the seat next to me, reaching for her glass of water with a shaky hand. Mr. and Mrs. Clark look so uncomfortable, they're trying to look at anything except my messed-up family. Even Jeremiah is avoiding making eye contact with anyone. They've never experienced Miller drama in such full force before.

After several very long minutes, Mom reaches across the table to grab an empty glass and a bottle of wine. She pours herself a hefty glass, then looks around sheepishly. "Well, it's already paid for. We might as well drink it."

* * *

There are about a thousand things running through my mind during the drive home. The first of which being, I can't believe how calmly my mom is taking this. This is probably the biggest bombshell that I've ever dropped on her, and she spent the entire dinner acting like we were out for a nice holiday meal with friends.

I'm pretty sure the only reason the Clarks even bothered to stay was because she was acting so calm. I assume she's just waiting until we're alone to unleash the tirade that's building up inside her. The entire drive home I prepare my defense, coming up with a list of reasons why Jer and me having a baby isn't the absolute worst thing in the world.

Number One: We love each other.

Number Two: We were already planning on getting married after college, so this is really just a time frame shift, rather than a complete derailment of plans.

Number Three: Jeremiah will stay close for school, so he can help with the baby. We'll be able to stagger our classes, so he can watch the baby while I'm in school and vice versa. We'll still get our degrees, it just might take longer.

Number Four: We really do love each other.

Even so, I can hear the "Dad fight" brewing. And honestly, after tonight, I'm feeling pretty angry with Dad as well.

I've done so much preparing for the argument I know is coming, that I'm already cracking my knuckles and opening my mouth to present my first argument when we walk in the door. But instead of letting me have it, Mom just sinks into the sofa, picks up her knitting, and starts casting on stitches.

I gape. "What are you doing?"

"Knitting."

I fold my arms. "You're not going to yell at me? Tell me how irresponsible I'm being? Tell me I've ruined my life?"

She shrugs. "Do you want me to?"

"Well, no," I gasp, "but I mean… c'mon. Your sixteen-year-old daughter is pregnant. Doesn't that make you mad?"

She sighs, not looking at me. "It makes me feel a lot of things, Dani. Worried. Sad. Scared, and yes, even a little mad."

I look down.

"But what good would it do to yell at you? When I suspect you've already felt all these things and more."

A tear rolls down my cheek and plops on the hard wood floor. How did she know?

Waning Gibbous

Before I know it, Mom has me scheduled for an appointment with her OB-GYN. How she got me in so fast, I'll never know. But the next Monday, there I am, sitting in the waiting room of Dr. Henderson, the very same Dr. Henderson who apparently delivered me.

There's something really weird about the doctor who delivered me as a baby now doing the same for me. But it's a small town. Not a lot of options.

The waiting room at Dr. Henderson's could not be any more different from the women's clinic if it tried. First of all, instead of the sterile, empty blue walls at the clinic, Dr. Henderson's are painted pale pink, and large-scale artistic portraits of newborns hang every few feet. The couches are soft and comfortable, not like the hard plastic I sat on a month earlier, and the end tables are overflowing with magazines—new editions too—about parenthood, pregnancy, or home living. All very upper middle class. The fluorescent lights have been replaced with soft bulbs which cast a soothing glow over every surface.

The whole place feels both welcoming and overwhelmingly feminine. Not to mention that everyone here looks content. That's the difference between being happily pregnant versus "knocked up." The women here—most of them in their late twenties or early thirties—look happy to be pregnant.

A few of them eye me with judgment on their faces, no doubt wondering how old I am. My high school hoodie can only hide the baby bump so much. And yeah, I've developed a bump. I'm not sure how much longer I can get by in school before someone figures it out.

Even so, I feel at ease in the waiting room. I scroll through social media posts on my phone, occasionally clicking on a personality test, even though I know it's click bait and it's not like I really need to know which movie princess I am.

The one that gets pregnant, whichever one that is.

We only wait about fifteen minutes before the nurse calls my name.

"Do you want me to come back with you?" Mom asks. It's a question I've been mulling over for days. How much do I let Mom be a part of this with me? We've never exactly been close, but some part of me feels like there are some things a daughter needs her mom for. Buying a prom dress, getting married, having a baby. Not necessarily in that order.

"Yeah," I reply, "If you don't mind."

She looks as surprised as I feel, but she sets down her magazine all the same and follows me down the hall.

This time, I come prepared. I've been drinking water all day, so much that Shelby even commented. "Oh Dani, you must be really *thirsty*." The emphasis on the word "thirsty" implies that I'm wanting something more than water.

When the nurse tells me to leave a urine sample, I've got plenty to give. Once I'm finished, I meet Mom in the examination room where the nurse checks all my vitals, blood pressure, heart rate, etc. Then she tells me to lay back so she can get a reading of the baby's heartbeat. She calls it a baby, not a pregnancy. Another big difference from the women's clinic.

Once she's done, Mom and I wait around for Dr. Henderson to show up. Mom tries to keep up small talk, asking me about how school was that day, what I learned, all those parent questions that she has to ask, but Dr. Henderson takes so long that she runs out of things to talk about.

After we run through her list of questions, we sit in silence for a while. So awkward. It's bad enough I start to wish I'd left her in the waiting room. Mom starts humming under her breath. She only knows one tune. I don't even know what the song is called. All I know is that ever since I was a baby, Mom has hummed the same tune. She used to hum it to me when I trying to fall asleep, so I developed a Pavlovian response every time I heard it.

Sure enough, my eyelids start to droop and I lay back on the patient table, ready to fall asleep. Well, if Dr. Henderson is going to make me wait forever, I might as well take a nap, right?

Just as I'm about to drift off, the door opens. My eyes fly open.

"Well, well, well, Danielle Miller!" Dr. Henderson says after the door latches behind her. "Seems like just a few years ago, I was watching you come into this world, and now look at you! Surprise pregnancy!"

I scowl.

Dr. Henderson settles onto the rolling stool between the patient table where I'm stuck halfway between lying down and sitting fully up. I'm not really sure where she wants me. Am I supposed to lay down and get poked and prodded some more?

She gives the stool a good spin before wheeling it over to talk to me. Even though she looks like she's about sixty years old, she's got way more energy than anyone I've ever met. She could give Mr. Craig a run for his money. I get the feeling Dr. Henderson is one of those people who can't sit still. Makes me wonder how she ever made it through medical school. But Mom swears she's great, and I don't have a lot of choice.

"So," she says, looking at my chart, "your urine test came back fine. Nothing to worry about there. What's your diet like?"

I shrug. "Um, well, there for a while, I couldn't hardly eat anything. Because I was always throwing up."

"Yes. Well we're at fifteen weeks now. Has that settled down?"

I nod. "Yeah, now I feel like I'm always hungry. So I eat just about everything."

"That's pretty normal." She barely takes a breath as she launches into her obviously memorized from overuse speech. "Some things to avoid: lunch meat, because it's high in sodium. Caffeine. You can have one cup of coffee a day, if you need it."

My heart sinks. No more soda.

She keeps talking. "Soft cheeses, you run the risk of listeria infections. The newest studies say sushi is okay, but don't overdo it and avoid high-mercury fishes."

"Okay."

"No alcohol, no smoking, no drugs."

I roll my eyes. What kind of person does she think I am?

Mom interrupts. "Dr. Henderson has to say that to all patients, Dani."

Dr. Henderson looks up. "Yup." She rattles over several more instructions about what to expect in the coming weeks and to make another appointment. "Do you have any questions?"

"Can I get out of PE?" I ask, jokingly.

Mom raises an eyebrow at me, but Dr. Henderson chuckles. "The most recent studies say you can continue the level of exercise that you were accustomed to before becoming pregnant. So, long story short. No. You can't. But if you start to feel dizzy or nauseated, then stop what you're doing immediately." She pauses for half a second before dropping a bombshell on me. "Also, we'll need to take some blood before you leave."

My eyes bulge. "Blood? Why?" And how come Mom didn't warn me that I was going to get stuck with needles today?

The doctor smiles indulgently. "Standard stuff really. We can measure your hormone levels, check for drug usage and STIs." Sexually transmitted infections.

"I don't do drugs. And I definitely don't have an STI."

She stands up. "I'm afraid it's required." She pulls my chart off of her clipboard and hands it to me. Me. Not Mom. Now that's something. She opens the door. "Have a nice day."

Great.

I look over at Mom, but she's too busy gathering her things to notice. She slings her purse over her shoulder. "Well, off we go."

"I don't want to have my blood drawn." I know I sound like a baby, but I absolutely hate needles.

Mom sighs. "Would it help if I was there with you?"

"Not really."

"Would it help if I told you that you will get stuck with several more needles before this whole ordeal is over?"

My mouth drops open. "What? Why?"

"That's just how it is."

I climb off the table. "That's stupid. Women have been having babies for centuries. Why do they suddenly have to make it so horrible by adding needles?"

Mom snorts. "Trust me, by the time you're done, you won't think the needles are the most painful part."

I freeze mid-step. Childbirth is painful. All this time I've been seeing myself with a baby, hoping it looks like Jeremiah, and not once did I ever think about the fact that childbirth is painful. Man, I feel stupid. Weeks of being pregnant and never really putting two and two together.

Mom realizes why I'm upset. She rubs my back. "Dani, it's okay. You'll get through it."

"But what if I can't?"

"You will," she says, "and if it's too painful, you can get an epidural. Trust me, you can do this. Like you said, women have been having babies for centuries. If they can do it, you can too."

"I don't know…" My heart is racing.

"You can, and you will. You have months to prepare for this. And by the time it happens…" She looks me square in the eye. "You'll be ready. I promise. Mother Nature has a way of preparing us for this. It's her gift to women everywhere."

That calms me more than anything. Mom never talks about Mother Nature like that, like Granny does. She doesn't do the New Age nature-worship stuff like Granny. She's a perfect little middle-class suburbanite. She doesn't fit in with the hippies. But when she says that, I wonder if maybe some part of her still believes in how Granny raised her, still holds onto the things she was taught as a child about the forces of Nature and sisterhood and all that.

Who knows? But it's enough to get me through the blood draw.

And maybe Mom is right. Maybe Mother Nature does have a plan for me. Why else would I have felt drawn to Jeremiah that afternoon in August?

I think about that night at the beach, when we wandered off. It was so perfect. And I think maybe the Moon and the Ocean and Earth herself were watching over me. And if they wanted me to be with Jeremiah and to have this baby, who am I to argue?

New Moon

It turns out, I was right to worry about the kids at school noticing my growing belly. That, and the fact that I've ditched my usual jeans for sweat pants the past few weeks. I guess I wasn't hiding it as well as I thought.

I start to notice how every time I enter a classroom, the other students break off talking. And I'm attracting some stares. And whispers.

The whispers are the worst, because on some level, I'd rather they just come right out and ask me, instead of staring at me in the hallway and then speculating with their friends.

I've taken to trying to hide my belly whenever I'm standing. When Jeremiah and I are chatting at his locker, I make sure to stand so that I'm halfway behind him at all times. Even that's not enough. I overhear the senior girl who has the locker three down from Jer whispering to her friend. "Oh, she definitely is. Look, you can tell."

When I glance over, she has the decency to pretend she wasn't looking at me. But I'm not stupid. I know.

When I unpack my lunch in the cafeteria, one of the girls at the next table makes a comment about watching what I eat, and my ears get hot with embarrassment.

Shelby glares. "Why don't you shut up, Beth!"

"Shelby, stop!" I hiss. Jeremiah drapes a protective arm around my shoulders.

"What?" she asks, "I'm defending you."

"You'll just make it worse. I don't need you drawing attention to me."

She snorts. "Trust me, you're getting the attention. No matter how much you want to avoid it." She shrugs and takes a bite of her food, chewing dramatically before swallowing. "I say embrace it, make it your own."

* * *

Never have I longed for Winter Break more than this year. By now the whole school has figured it out, even though I've only officially told Jeremiah and Shelby. It's pretty common knowledge that Dani Miller got herself pregnant. I can't tell if they think I'm an idiot or a slut or both. Which is pretty funny, since I've only ever slept with Jeremiah a few times, and it took me months of internal debate before I even did that.

The good news is, I'm feeling so much less sick. I feel healthy now, just a little rounder than usual.

The bad news is, it's the week of the Winter Bake Sale, and Mom is doubling down on her insistence that I need to help her prepare. She's got a ridiculously long list of treats to make and we end up spending all Saturday working on them. Between each batch, she offers little remarks about how every mother should know her way around the kitchen and don't I appreciate all that she's teaching me?

Not really. My kid's going to eat Oreos like a normal person.

By the time we're done, we have boxes of cupcakes, brownies, cookies, scones, everything. If it's ever been baked in an oven, we made it today. I'm exhausted, but Mom is as chipper as ever. She wipes floury hands on her apron and leans on the counter across from me. "What do you want for dinner?"

"We've been cooking all day."

Mom pulls her apron off. "We'll go out. Whatever you want."

"Really?"

Strictly speaking, Mom's not a huge fan of going out. She says anything that a restaurant can make, she can make better and cheaper. Plus, she hates giving money to the corporations. She's got a whole tirade about it, the importance of supporting local places instead of international conglomerates. I've heard it dozens of time, usually right after I complain about some new gadget Shelby bought. I have no interest in hearing it again.

I rack my brain for an idea. "How about that Italian place over close to Jeremiah's house?"

Her eyes crinkle, and I know she approves. That place is owned by actual Italian immigrants, and the food is to die for. "Sounds perfect."

Waxing Crescent

The bake sale is a week-long extravaganza. They set up a booth in the cafeteria so kids can buy desserts during lunch, then they have it open every evening until 7 pm. All the Booster Club moms take it in rotation, which days and times they'll oversee the booth. Everyone serves at least once.

On Monday, Mom drives with me to school so we can unload all of her pastries first thing in the morning. We're walking our third load of boxes in when Mrs. Vicks stops us just outside the Booster Club's office.

"I'm so sorry, Mrs. Miller," she begins.

My mom's lips tighten. She hates being called by Dad's name. "I go by Roth now, please. Or just Hannah."

"Of course, well," she pauses and glances pointedly at me, "We really don't need any more baked goods."

Mom blinks, then looks at me. "Dani, why don't you head to class? You'd hate to be late for homeroom."

I lower the boxes to the bench next to me and pretend to leave, but as soon as I'm around the corner, I stop and lean back against the wall.

Mom's voice stays low and calm. "What's this about?"

"Well, given your daughter's *situation*..." I can almost see Mrs. Vick's smirk as she talks. "We thought maybe you were taking on a little too much around here. If you're struggling to focus on your family. I mean... your daughter is clearly begging for attention."

"Excuse me?"

"Why else would she have gotten herself into this predicament?" Her voice is syrupy sweet, but in that deceptive way so you know you're about to be stabbed in the back.

Mom sees right through it. "It was an accident."

"Sure, sure." Mrs. Vick smacks her gum so loud I can hear it around the corner. "An accident that could probably have been avoided if her mother hadn't been so busy with her work. Feeding starving children halfway across the world, all the while ignoring your own. And now look at her."

Behind the corner, I fume. What a load of bullshit. So apparently kids with stay at home moms don't get knocked up? Mrs. Vick is way out of line. I'm about ready to storm back over there and give her a piece of my mind, but Mom does it first.

"Don't talk about my daughter that way."

"Of course," Mrs. Vick simpers. "I'm sorry. That said, we are all booked up. We don't need your help."

"Well, if that's how you feel," Mom says coolly, "then I guess I'll just go."

And with that, she leaves. She breezes around the corner where I'm hiding, and I press myself to the wall to avoid being seen. Good thing I've got so much practice being invisible. Mom doesn't even notice me as she walks by. Her head is held high, and her arms are empty. Ha, she left the boxes of brownies for Mrs. Vicks to deal with. Go her!

I peer around the corner and watch Mrs. Vicks struggle with all the boxes. At first, she tries to stack them all on top of each other, then lifts them, but the stack is too high and she can't see around it. So then she just leaves them all on the bench and walks away. I keep watching until I see her come back with a large wheeled garbage bin. My jaw drops.

I can't believe what she's about to do. All that hard work, the hours in the kitchen, thrown away just like that. It makes me want to cry as I watch her lift every last one of the boxes my mom and I brought and toss them into the trash. Not just the ones from our last trip, but she actually goes into the Booster Club office and pulls out the previous boxes.

I'm livid.

I debate storming over there and giving her a piece of my mind, but the tardy bell rings, and I dash for my classroom instead. All morning, I fume. I go back and forth in my head. Should I say something or would that just make things worse? I'm so upset, Jeremiah says something as he walks with me between classes.

"Hey, what's up with you?"

"What do you mean?" Master of denial, that's me.

He doesn't fall for it. "You've been upset all morning. Something's wrong. Is it the…" he drops his voice. "the baby?"

I roll my eyes. "No need to pretend like it's a secret now, Jer. The whole school has figured it out."

"Really?"

Then I tell him all about what happened between Mrs. Vicks and my mom this morning. By the time I'm done, my voice is shaking and I'm fighting tears.

He's flabbergasted. "She threw them all away?"

I recognize the look of longing in his eyes. No one admires my mom's baking more than my boyfriend. It's a good thing he uses up so much energy with Tae Kwon Do, because he will eat anything my mom puts in front of him. I bet he had been planning all weekend what to buy.

"Yeah, just tossed them right in."

He groans. "That's so messed up."

"I know!" I cross my arms. "Should I say something?"

"Honestly?" he asks.

I nod.

Jer shakes his head. "I don't think so. I mean, it wouldn't change anything, right?"

"She has to know that what she did is wrong!"

"But would she listen to you?"

He has a good point. I'm not exactly the most persuasive speaker. In fact, I'm kind of a mess when it comes to public speaking or confrontation or anything that involves speaking my mind.

My shoulders slump. "I guess not."

"Sometimes, you just have to let things go. Pick your battles." More Tae Kwon Do philosophy, but it's good advice. I nod my head and wrap my arms around his neck, pulling him in for a kiss.

When we finish, he leans his forehead on mine. "I'm sorry," he whispers. "It's not fair."

Then again, when has life ever been fair?

I try to forget all about the brownie incident, but when I see Mrs. Vicks standing at the Booster Club's bake sale booth, peddling sub-par treats, it all comes rushing back. I almost storm over there, but when I pass by, she gets a look in her eye, like she's just stepped on a slug or something, and I can't bring myself to do it.

* * *

When I get home after school, Mom's on the phone with someone and pacing around the living room. I can tell by the way she walks, heavy on the heels, that she's upset, and I tiptoe toward the stairs. I'm halfway up when I hear my name.

"You don't have a right to judge Dani, or me, or anyone."

I pause and peer over the banister.

"No, Cheryl, this situation doesn't involve you!" Cheryl is Mrs. Vicks's first name.

Long pause.

"So that's just it, huh? My daughter gets pregnant and I'm off the Booster Club? You can't risk your precious little image? Screw your image." My eyebrows shoot up. Mom does not talk like that.

Another pause.

My mom stops in front of the fireplace. "Go to hell, you catty, self-righteous bitch!" She hangs up, then throws the phone across the room. Luckily, it hits the couch and falls onto the soft cushion.

"Whoa, Mom..."

Her head snaps up. "Oh, sweetheart. I didn't realize you were home."

"Are you okay?"

"Yeah," she sighs. "Yeah, just fine. Um... do you want some dinner?"

Yes, I'm starving. I'm always starving these days. I creep down the stairs. "If you're too busy, I can..."

"No, not too busy. Not at all." She bustles into the kitchen and starts pulling out pans. "Does tomato soup and grilled cheese sound good?"

I nod. Sounds perfect, especially as the weather gets cooler and the days shorter. Tomato soup and grilled cheese is my go-to comfort food. Must be Mom's as well. I settle onto the stool at the counter and watch her work. She can make just about anything with her eyes closed, and she dances through the steps without a second thought. Fifteen minutes later, steam rises from a bowl of homemade tomato soup and warms my face.

"Thanks, Mom." I'm not even sure if I'm talking about the soup.

She kisses my temple. "Anything for you, baby."

First Quarter

For as long as I can remember, Mom has insisted on celebrating Christmas early. I get it, since Caleb died during right before Christmas. It's hard on her. But it's always been a little weird.

Before my parents divorced, Christmas was basically a week-long argument, complete with screaming and crying and eventually Dad walking out of the house.

After Dad left, Christmas dwindled. Part of the problem is that any religious or spiritual connection Mom had with the holiday died with Caleb. Not that she ever had much to begin with. Granny's always been a New Age hippy sort, and Mom was raised with goddesses and moon phases instead of Jesus and Mary.

Dad's more of a casual Christian, and that's how I was raised until he left and Mom gave up. I'm not even sure what she believes any more. If anything.

Without the religious necessities of celebrating Christmas, it really just boils down to giving each other gifts. This year, I really want to do something nice for Mom, especially after the fiasco with the Booster Club. I'm still reeling from hearing her cuss them out over the phone, but I'm also pretty proud of her.

Not to mention, it felt good that she was defending me.

Of course, my mom, Mrs. Selfless herself, refuses to answer me properly when I ask her what she wants. She gives me these little half answers like, "I just want to spend time with you, sweetie," and "If you insist on spending money, put it toward Earth's Bounty. We're hoping to build another well in Gambia."

I do end up giving some of my savings to Earth's Bounty but it still doesn't feel like enough, so the weekend before school lets out, I ask her if she wants to have a day out, just the two of us.

"I'd love that, Dani," she says. She actually looks like she means it. Maybe she's forgotten how little we have in common.

"Great," I say.

She climbs off of the sofa. "You'll be wanting some maternity clothes anyway."

I look down at my belly. It's true, I've definitely rounded out. The sweat pants and T-shirt look won't cut it much longer.

"Okay, I guess." I'm not exactly looking forward to the prospect of wearing maternity clothes. Last time I checked, new mothers weren't exactly the most stylish people in the world. Not that I've ever been particularly fashionable, but I try not to look like a thirty-year-old woman, if I have the chance.

Mom reads my expression. "I felt the same way. We'll find you something you like."

She's bordering on talking about Caleb, even indirectly. Pregnancy with Caleb, because I know she didn't buy any new clothes with me. Tiptoeing around the subject of Caleb. I'm not even sure what to say at this point. Mom's been freakishly nice to be me lately, basically since she found out I'm pregnant. Any other parent would flip out, Dad sure did, but Mom's taking it all in stride. It's like my pregnancy presents the challenge she's always needed to prove that she is, in fact, perfect.

Apparently, Mom's done her research, because she pulls out a notebook with a list of all the maternity shops in the area and starts mapping them out on her cell phone. I watch over her shoulder and try not to think about how I'm not even halfway done with being pregnant, but I've already failed this baby in so many ways. This kid deserves a nice organized mom, but instead it got me—a teen mom who never quite knows what's happening until it's already happened. Poor thing is doomed before it's even born.

Mom snaps her notebook shut and stands up. "Shall we get going?"

I wasn't really expecting that we were going to drop everything and head straight out. I was planning on spending most of the morning watching

Netflix and lazing around on the couch, but she's already slung her purse over her shoulder and is heading for the garage, so I race to catch up.

Thirty minutes later, we walk into the first shop. The sales consultants outnumber the customers, three to one, and we're not even fully in the door before one of them rushes over to us. "Hello, hello. What brings us in today?" She has one of those permanent smiles, and I can't help but stare at her teeth while she talks. Her lips never meet.

"Pregnancy," I grumble.

Mom places a hand on my shoulder. "Just shopping for some clothes for my daughter."

The sales lady practically squeals. "Oh, is this your first?"

I try stifle a laugh and fail. "Yeah."

"And how far along are you?"

I tell her. She looks positively giddy, and I can tell she's holding back from touching my stomach. That's probably rule number one of working in a maternity store. Don't pet the customers. She keeps peppering me with questions, but luckily Mom saves me.

"We'll just browse for a while, if that's okay."

"Of course, of course." Even though she's still bustling around us. She must work on commission.

Finding jeans is the hardest part. There are a handful of decent tops, high-waisted ones that tie in the back. Sure, they're a little frillier than I would normally wear, but at least they're solid colored.

The jeans, on the other hand…

Apparently, pregnancy is a second childhood or something, because all the jeans are embellished with these ridiculous glittering patterns. Flowers and butterflies. I feel like I'm six years old again.

"Don't they have any plain blue jeans?" I complain.

Mom holds up a promising pair, but sure enough, when she turns it around, it has flowers embroidered on the back pockets. "You may just have to make do with what they have."

"How much longer do you think I can go in just my sweat pants?"

She shrugs. "A couple months, probably."

I groan. Sweatpants are great and all, but I feel half-naked wearing them. But these jeans are just ridiculous. In the end, I agree to try on some of the least offensive sorts, but they still feel too girly and childish. Too cutesy.

"Do you want me to come in there with you?" Mom offers as she hands me the stack of clothes.

I wrinkle my nose. "No way."

She sighs. "I was just offering."

"Well it's weird."

Except, once I get in there, I see this big round pad that I guess I'm supposed to put around my stomach to see how the clothes will fit when I'm huge, but I can't seem to get it to sit in the right spot. It keeps falling too low or riding up too high, so I end up calling my mom in to help me.

She adjusts it for me, then hands me the first shirt, which I pull over my head.

"Now that's nice," she says.

She must be blind or something, because all I see is a hippopotamus swimming in a forest green tent. I'm huge. I yank the shirt off. Maybe the next shirt will look better.

It doesn't.

In fact, we go through half the stack before I yank the pillow off my stomach. "I look fat."

Mom blinks. "Well, no. You look pregnant."

I sink to the bench and lean my head on my hands. "What's the difference? Pregnant or fat? Either way, those clothes make me look disgusting."

Mom lifts up one of the shirts. "I thought this one was kind of sweet."

I peer up at her. "Is that really how big I'm going to get?" My voice cracks a little as I ask it.

She lowers the shirt to look at me. "Yeah, just about."

"Oh my god!" I bury my face in my knees. "I can't go to school looking like that!"

I can see Mom's toe tapping on the floor from between my arms. She's getting impatient. Normally, I'm not so dramatic, but I think, given the circumstances, I'm allowed a little drama.

Then, she sits next to me on the bench and puts an arm around my shoulders. "You don't just wake up huge, you know? It happens gradually, so slow you don't even really notice it. And it really is beautiful. It might not seem like it now, but it is."

A tear slides down my cheek, and I turn my head away from her so she can't see it. Even so, she leans over and pushes my hair away from my face. "Let's get the green one and the blue one. I think they looked the best with your complexion."

* * *

When we get home, I pull all the new clothes we bought before school started out of my closet. Mini-skirts and tight, high-waisted jeans chosen with Jeremiah in mind. When I hold them up, they seem tiny. No way I'll fit in them now. I may never fit in them again. Thin and pretty Danielle is a thing of the past. Some of these I only wore once, and it seems like such a waste to get rid of them now.

But what else can I do? I have to make room for my new clothes. I spend the afternoon folding and stacking them all into a cardboard box. Goodbye bare midriffs. Goodbye long legs. Goodbye enticing, beautiful woman. Like the moon, I am transitioning from lovely maiden to heavy mother. Up next, old crone.

When I finish, I carry the heavy box down the stairs and into the kitchen where Mom sits looking over Earth's Bounty paperwork. I grunt as I plop the box on an open chair.

Mom glances up. "What's this?"

"My old school clothes," I say. "The ones I'm too fat for now. I'm getting rid of them."

"Getting rid of them?" Mom repeats.

I shrug. "I'm never going to fit in them again. I figured I could donate them."

Mom cocks her head to the side, watching me carefully. "You don't know you'll never fit in them again." She stands up and picks up the box. "I say we store them in the basement for a while, see how you feel in a year."

I sink into the open chair. I'm still feeling gross from shopping. "Whatever, I'm not changing my mind."

Full Moon

Dad and I haven't exactly been on speaking terms since Thanksgiving. For one, he seems to think Jeremiah is some monstrously bad influence on me. The mere mention of my boyfriend makes my dad grit his teeth and refuse to look at me.

Mom's been supportive. Dad's been judgmental. To him, I'm a walking failure.

For another, bowling nights have been postponed indefinitely. According to Mom, I shouldn't be lifting heavy things. I could pull a muscle or hurt the baby. I remind her that bowling balls are only like ten pounds, but she won't have it. Dad suggested doing a movie instead, but I could tell his heart wasn't in it, so I just let him off the hook. Now I spend those Friday nights at home with Mom or Jeremiah.

Still, the custody agreement says I have to spend a week with him every year for Christmas, so the Saturday after school lets out, where am I? Standing outside his apartment door with my mom, waiting to be let in.

Mom's somber, and her normally flat-ironed coif hangs limp on her face. That's no surprise. While I spend a week with Dad every year, doing the traditional Christmas thing, she spends the week thinking about Caleb. Alone.

Mom doesn't want me around. It's the one week a year she allows herself to be anything less than perfect and she can't have any witnesses.

There are so many things I don't understand, that I want to ask but I'm too scared to know the truth. Why is it so much harder on her than it is for Dad? He lost a son too. Shouldn't he be a complete wreck, too? Maybe I just don't remember the first years—I was a baby, after all—but it seems like I've never seen Dad grieve for Caleb at all.

Then again, I've never seen Mom either. She shuttles me away for a week so I don't see it all. Every year, I come back and even though nothing in the house has changed at all, it feels different. Heavier, darker, sadder.

We arrive at Dad's place exactly three minutes before nine in the morning. Mom has this whole speech about punctuality. I've heard it about a million times. It's important to show up early to everything, but not too early, because that's rude. The sweet spot is five minutes. So technically we're two minutes late to being properly early.

She carried my suitcase all the way up the three flights of stairs to his apartment for me. Heavy lifting and all. Now though, she looks exhausted. Not her usual businesslike self. The sadness is starting already. Maybe my pregnancy reminds her too much of Caleb. Maybe she won't be able to get through this week. I start to offer to stay home, but she speaks before I have a chance to get a word out.

"Are you going to be okay?" she asks.

"Why wouldn't I be?" I ask defensively.

She purses her lips. "Well, you and your father haven't been getting along lately."

"He was a total jerk."

"You took us all by surprise, Dani. He's trying. I think you should forgive him." She pushes my hair out of my eyes. "No one behaves their best when they receive news like that."

"Bad news, you mean."

"Life-altering news."

I sigh. Life-altering is right. But it's my life being altered, not his. I glance at her. "You didn't act like that."

She smiles sadly and rests a hand on my stomach. "Children need to know they are loved. Even before they're born." Oh yeah, she's definitely already thinking about Caleb.

Before I can respond, she reaches over and presses the doorbell, and Dad answers in record time.

"Hello, Dani-lion!"

He yanks me into a huge bear hug, complete with a loud smacking kiss on the cheek. "How's my baby girl doing?" Dad is too busy petting me, so Mom has to lift the suitcase into the apartment by herself.

"I'm fine," I mumble, pulling away. Dad's putting on a show. He wants to pretend like nothing's different. But he's going to have a hard time of it. I'm pretty round. At this point, no one is looking at me and thinking that maybe I just ate too many tacos. It's obvious I'm pregnant.

Dad avoids the issue by not looking at me. He breezes through the front hallway and into the living area where Ashley is already waiting with a sorry attempt at brunch on the kitchen table. She should have known better than to try. No one cooks like my mom.

I glance back at my mom, and I guess I look extra pitiful, because she gives me a tight squeeze. "Be good, mind your manners, and don't get into any arguments with your father."

It was too much to hope that I could escape.

Waning Gibbous

Things aren't so bad for the first few days. Dad is obviously uncomfortable around me. He can't sit still. When I enter the room, he goes from relaxing in his armchair to buzzing around like a really annoying bumblebee. I spend most of the week hanging out on the sofa, texting Jeremiah and Shelby.

Or, attempting to text Jeremiah and Shelby.

Here's the problem. Shelby is away on her yearly cruise through the Caribbean. Her parents are loaded. They used to go without her, but now that she's fairly self-sufficient, she goes along. From what I've heard, she spends most of the time making out with any cute boy who looks her way, and only ever sees her parents for meals.

It sounds delightful.

Jeremiah is on the senior ski trip. This pill is a little harder to swallow, kind of like the huge pre-natal multivitamins Mom is forcing down my throat every morning. For the longest time, I thought Jeremiah wasn't going to go on the trip. He even told me he wasn't going to go. Then, at the last minute, he decides to turn in his paperwork, because he "wants to hang out with his friends."

And that's the real kicker. Because I've been with Jeremiah for over a year now, and I'm only just realizing that I have no idea who he hangs out with when he's not with me. That's something I should know. But, we don't have any classes together, because his are all senior level courses, and I'm a year behind. And every time we go out with friends, we go out with Shelby and Miles. I guess I thought that was all the friends he had. But now he's talking about these guys that he's known since he was in grade school, and I feel like

I've been missing out on this huge part of his life. It makes me wonder what else I've missed. Or what else he hasn't told me.

He's been impossible to reach all week.

That is, he gives me these little check-in texts. Things like "having fun, but miss you" and "hope you're doing good." They feel empty, meaningless. Not like him.

Case in point. Christmas morning, I sleep in as late as I can, because I don't really want to see Dad yet, and Jeremiah texts me, "Merry Christmas. Hope it's a good one."

Seriously? He could have sent that to his grandmother.

The alarm clock on the nightstand next to me reads 10:30. I can't hide the entire day in here. Dad will come find me eventually. He's never really learned to respect my privacy. So even though I close the door to the ultra-beige guest room, he still comes in whenever he wants. He knocks, then opens the door without waiting for an answer. Sometimes, I wonder if Caleb was still alive, if he would do the same to him.

It's stupid to wonder. Caleb isn't alive, and there's no way of knowing.

I plod down the hallway to the living room, where he and Ashley are already snuggling on the sofa, laughing over something. Groan. I need to announce my presence and fast, before I see something I can't unsee.

"Hey."

They immediately push away from each other, scattering to the opposite ends of the sofa. Smooth.

Dad jumps up. "Merry Christmas, baby girl. Do you want some waffles? Ashley made them!"

I turn to look toward the kitchen, where sure enough, a plate of soggy looking waffles is waiting on the counter, untouched. "No thanks."

"Well here, come on in, join the fun. We waited for you."

"Thanks." I plop onto the armchair across from them and run a hand over the small mound of my belly. It's becoming a habit. Sit down, rub belly.

Dad can't hide his frown. "How about I pass out the gifts this year?" He doesn't wait for an answer, but starts digging around beneath the tree. Once all the presents are passed out, he settles back onto the sofa, this time noticeably closer to Ashley and puts an arm around her. They both stare at me.

I guess I'm opening my gifts with an audience. I sigh and rip open the paper, but my eyes widen when I see what's inside. "Whoa, a laptop?"

"Ashley thought you'd like it," Dad jumps in, "because you like to write so much." He stands and walks over, already pulling the box out of my hands. "This is state-of-the-art. It's got loads of memory and an excellent processor. It's lightweight, so you can take it to school with you."

"We're not allowed to have laptops at school," I say, but he doesn't hear me.

"And it comes with an OLED display, a high-res screen…" he rambles on. I start to open the rest of my gifts while he talks. He's already pulling the laptop out of the box and setting it up. All the rest of my gifts are laptop accessories—a case, software, a wireless mouse.

When he's finished running the startup, he hands it back to me to create a password. "I was thinking, you could start submitting your poetry to places. Maybe make a few extra bucks?"

I glance up at him. "Thanks, Dad."

He gives me a squeeze. "Don't mention it."

It really is such a nice gift, way nicer than anything I got either of them. But it feels like too much. I close the lid and watch them open their gifts. The usual things. Clothes, movies, I bought Dad a back massager I found at the mall last time Shelby and I went shopping. It's lame, but he likes dumb gadgets like that. Ashley got a gift certificate to a salon. I have no idea what she likes, and I honestly don't care.

We save the stockings for last. Dad makes hot apple cider for each of us, then hands the stockings around. Mine is mostly candy, which sucks, because lately sugar has started to give me heartburn which Mom says is only going to get worse. Just great.

Dad's stocking rests on the sofa next to him, forgotten, because his eyes are trained on Ashley as she opens hers.

She digs around, pulling out various things, nail polishes, candy, hand creams, then at the very bottom.

My jaw drops, and I'm not the only one. She looks up sharply. "What's this, Bert?"

My dad kneels on the floor in front of her, takes the box from her hands and opens it. "Ashley…" he begins.

This cannot be happening.

He keeps speaking. "You've brought so much joy into my life. Joy like I've never known before."

I frown. Hard not to take that personally.

"And, I'd like you to become a permanent part of my family." He locks eyes with Ashley. "Will you marry me?"

Kill.

Me.

Now.

I stare open-mouthed as Ashley bursts into tears and grabs the box from Dad's hands. She nods emphatically as she slides the ring onto her finger. "Yes!" Shocking, considering she's only been waiting for this moment for three years now.

They throw themselves on each other, hugging and kissing, and I've become invisible. Not the good kind of invisible, but the bad kind. Like suddenly I start to wonder if their lives would be so much better without me in it.

They don't even notice when I grab my phone and head back down the hallway to my room. Once I'm alone, I dial Mom's number. I know I shouldn't. I know alone time is important to her, but I need someone to talk to. Someone else who will be just as upset as I am.

"Dani?" she answers, "Are you okay?"

"Yeah," I grumble, "just…"

"Did something happen?"

I give a loud sigh. "Dad just asked Ashley to marry him."

"Oh." She goes silent for a few seconds. "Wow."

"Yeah."

She doesn't say anything for a while, but I can tell she's thinking a lot of things, and none of them particularly nice. When she does speak again, she says simply, "Well, tell him I said congratulations."

"Yeah," I mutter. We sit on either ends of the phone, neither talking, for a long time.

Finally, she breaks the silence. "Is there something else the matter?"

"When did Dad start cheating on you?"

She huffs into the phone. "What a question, Dani. Where did that come from?"

I'm terrified to actually say the words out loud, but I know she'll pull them out of me eventually. "Jeremiah and I haven't really talked in a week. He's been gone on that ski trip, but I guess I thought he would at least give me a call or something."

"He's still gone? I thought the seniors all came back yesterday morning."

My heart drops. "What?"

"Yeah," she says, "The school wouldn't keep them over Christmas. Parents want to spend that time with their kids." Normal parents. Not her.

"Oh." I can't think of anything else to say.

Her voice gets all serious, like it does when she's getting annoyed at my drama. I can almost see her smiling indulgently at me. "Be patient with him. He's going through a big change too right now."

"But what if he's breaking up with me?" I ask. "I don't want to do this all by myself."

"You'd be surprised, Dani, the kind of strength you have inside you. You'll see. You can do this." She pauses, then adds, "and you won't be alone."

Waning Crescent

"Look, I'm sorry," Jeremiah groans as he props his feet up on my mom's coffee table. "Like I said, I was busy with family stuff, and I figured you were too."

"I'm just saying, you could have called. I missed you." I reach over and slide my hand across the back of his shoulders, but he shrugs me off.

Ouch.

I scoot back to my own side of the sofa. "How was the ski trip?"

"Good."

I blink. "That's it? Good?"

"Good," he repeats, "it was fun. What else do you want me to say, Dani? What's with the third degree?"

"I'm just trying to have a conversation." I fold my arms and glare at the fireplace, anything to avoid looking at Jer.

We sit in silence for a couple minutes, then Jeremiah crosses the distance and wraps an arm around me. "Hey, c'mon. Why all the anger today? It can't be good for the baby." And to settle his point, he presses his hand to my growing baby bump. No way I'm going to be able to hide this when I go back to school. I'll be breaking out those maternity jeans soon enough.

I shrug. "Sometimes I just worry that you don't want to be with me anymore."

"What?" he cries, a little too emphatically. "No! I love you. You're acting crazy."

I don't think it's crazy, but I'm also not so sure it's worth an argument. An argument that might tip the scales and send him running for the hills.

I smile and nod. "Sorry."

And just like that, everything is solved. Jeremiah grabs the remote and flips on the television, cycling through the Netflix options without even consulting me until he finds a promising movie. Then he settles back into his cushion and throws an arm over my shoulders. Within seconds, his mind is already on something else. He's completely zoned into the movie, some old-timey Western I couldn't care less about if I tried. I curl my feet underneath me and lean against him, trying to relax enough to catch a quick nap. I'm always so tired these days, and the lack of caffeine only makes it worse.

I've completely fallen asleep by the time the movie is over, and Jeremiah shakes me awake. "Hey, I didn't realize you were napping down there."

I blink a few times to wake up. "Yeah, sorry."

"No big deal." He slides out from underneath me and stands up. "I might head on home anyway."

"Oh," I sigh. So much for a fun afternoon together. Napping on the sofa, so romantic.

"Yeah, well my mom wants me to watch the kids while she goes grocery shopping."

"Oh," I repeat.

He grabs his coat off the hook by the door and slides it on.

"Um, before you go…" I say.

"Yeah?"

"My next doctor's appointment is on Friday, at nine."

"Okay…" His eyes dart ever so slightly to the side, like he's impatient to get going.

I stand and follow him to the doorway. "Well, it's the ultrasound, so we can find out the sex of the baby."

"Oh," he says, his lips curling ever so slightly into a smile. "Cool."

The half-smile gives me hope. "Yeah, um well, I was hoping you could be there."

"Yeah," he agrees immediately, then pulls open the door. "Just text me details." Then he's off, down the steps to his car without another word.

I lean against the door frame and watch him go. "Bye…"

Waning Crescent

Friday morning, I'm back in Dr. Henderson's waiting room. Mom sits beside me with a notebook open on her lap, an entire sheet filled with questions about my pregnancy. Questions down to the stupidest detail, like should I be eating more iron-rich vegetables. She must have been jotting down notes about my diet (too sugary), my fluid consumption (not enough), and my sleep patterns (should I be sleeping on my back or my side?) for the past few weeks. I glare at the list shake my head with frustration. Just in time for her to write another question. "Techniques for managing anger? Yoga?"

For the love of… I pull out my phone and text Jeremiah. "Are you on your way?"

He responds automatically. "Can't come. Busy at home. Sorry."

"This is important!"

"Sorry. Family stuff."

I'm fuming as I type out. "This baby is your family! You should be here!"

But all I get back in return is another "Sorry."

I throw my phone back in my purse, hard enough for my mom to turn in her seat. "What's wrong?"

"Jer's not coming," I snap.

"Ah, I'm sorry."

I snort. "So is he, supposedly."

She starts to say "I'm sorry" again, but I cut her off with a glare. I don't need pity right now. I need my boyfriend.

Getting an ultrasound at Dr. Henderson's office is an entirely different experience than getting one at the women's health clinic. For one, the room looks more like a living room that just happens to have high-tech equipment in it than like an actual doctor's office. Mom sinks into the squishy sofa and turns her attention to the wide, flat screen on the wall. I'm not so lucky. I climb onto the exam table in the middle of the room.

The technician verifies my name and birthdate, then smiles indulgently at me. "So, big day, huh? Are we finding out the sex?" She is friendlier than the technician at the women's clinic.

I glance at the empty space next to Mom, then nod. "Yeah, I guess so."

"Well, if you're not sure," she says as she pulls the tube of gel out of a warmer and squirts it on my bare belly, "we can always put the pictures in an envelope and let you decide later."

"I'll think about it."

The picture pops up on the screen and my jaw drops. This picture looks a thousand times more human than the last one. And the picture quality is better too. It's a baby. A real baby.

Mom covers her mouth with her hand. "Oh, wow."

"Mom, you've done this before."

"I know… it's just…" she sighs and shakes her head. If I didn't know any better, I'd say she's about ready to cry, but my mom does not cry.

The actual ultrasound takes forever. The technician runs through a ton of measurements, head size, heart rate, and so on. She takes pictures of every single side of the baby, so at the end, there's a string of pictures of the baby's profile, legs, arms, face, and finally…

"Moment of truth, Mama," she says, "do you want to see the sex?"

I turn to look at Mom, but she shakes her head. "She means you, Dani. You're the mom."

"Oh, duh." I'm the mom. I'm the one in charge for once. And at this point, I don't really care if Jeremiah gets mad at me because I found out before him. I turn to the technician, "yeah, let's find out."

She shifts the sensor on my stomach and the picture changes. "Baby girl!"

I bite my lip, tears welling in the corners of my eyes. I turn to look at Mom, and she's choked up too. She pulls a tissue from her purse and dabs her eyes.

"It's a girl," I whisper.

"Yes, *she* is."

"Wow."

Mom stands up and gives me a side hug. "She's beautiful, Dani."

The technician snaps another picture, hits print, then cuts them, and hands the stack to me. "Something to show your friends." Yeah, like my friends want to see my big mistake.

"Thanks."

* * *

On the way home, Mom pulls into the parking lot of her favorite yarn shop. Most people just shop at Hobby Lobby, but Mom hates the place. She got super offended during the whole Obamacare debacle, quoted Granny with "when one woman suffers, we all suffer," then refused to shop there ever since. She likes this place better because the woman who owns the shop lives in town and even spins and dyes her own yarn, as well as sells some of the national brands. It's actually pretty cool, or it would be, if I knew anything about knitting.

I follow Mom into the store. The walls are shelved floor to ceiling, and the shelves are packed with colors and textures. I want to run my hand along each skein as I walk, feeling the differences in softness.

Mom goes straight to the pastels in the back. "I was waiting until we found out what you were having to start the blanket, but now that we know…" she picks up a skein of pale purple. "Do you like?"

"Mom, you don't have to make it something."

"Her," she corrects me, "and of course I do. It's tradition."

"Tradition?"

She nods. "My grandmother knit my baby blanket, and my mom made one for both you and Caleb. Now, it's my turn."

I scoff. "The tradition stops with you. I don't even know how to knit."

She flips the skein over to look at the yardage. "Let's see, 350 yards per skein, and I'll probably need about a thousand…" she raises her eyebrow while she adds. She grabs two more skeins, then looks at me. "Why don't you grab something? I'll teach you how to make a scarf. It's the easiest thing to start on."

I look around the room, finally settling on some charcoal gray with flecks of gold. I can make something for Jeremiah. The gold will match the flecks in his eyes.

Mom purses her lips like she wants to say something. I bet she knows I'm planning on giving the scarf to Jeremiah, but she ultimately nods her approval and we walk to the counter together.

During the rest of the drive, I pull the pictures out of my pocket and rifle through them. I linger on each picture. Even the silly ones, like the one of her foot, look so perfect. I trace the edges of her face with my finger. My baby. I'm going to have a baby. I still can't believe it. But there she is, in black and white.

My baby girl.

New Moon

The following Monday, I return to school, which means returning to Mr. Craig's homeroom. The first thing he does is arrange the desks in yet another Community Circle. Sigh.

He settles onto a stool and clasps his hands together as he leans over his knees. "Welcome back. One semester down, and another to go. And then, my inquisitive young people, you will be…" he pauses for dramatic effect, looking each one of us in the eye before continuing, "seniors." A few snickers go up around the circle.

Seniors.

It's like a light at the end of a tunnel. The possibility of escape after all these long torturous years of public education.

"But first," he says, "tell me about your breaks. Where did you go? Who did you see? Did you travel? Any good news? Any bad? Who wants to start?"

Mr. Craig has a way of rattling off questions so fast that I have a hard time processing it. Luckily, most of the other students can keep up. A few kids answer with their usual stuff. "Went to my grandma's house, ate some ham, got a new Playstation!"

Then it's my turn. I stare at my desk. "I usually spend Christmas with my dad. Um… he got me a laptop, which was pretty cool." I start to say I'm finished, then I add suddenly, "Oh, and I had an ultrasound. I found out I'm having a girl."

It's the first time I've really talked about the pregnancy in the Community Circle. Even though everyone knows I am. I've been pretty shut down about it. I'm not sure why I shared, except what's the point of hiding it?

The circle is silent for a few seconds, then a girl across the circle asks, "Do you have pictures?"

I look up and smile. "Yeah! In my backpack." I lean over and dig around for a few seconds before pulling out the best one. The one I was going to hang in my locker. She's curled around herself, and her nose and lips form this perfect little pout. I smile down at it for half a second, then pass it around the circle.

Most of the boys just glance at it then pass it on, but the girls are ecstatic. They crowd around each other and point and say things like, "look at that nose!" or "She's so cute!"

Normally, I would hate the attention, except this time, it's directed at a picture and not at me. And it's pretty cool to hear how girls I've barely spoken to my entire life are suddenly interested in something I'm doing.

Things come to a jarring halt though, when Shelby plucks the picture out of her neighbor's hands, holds it up to the light and says, "huh, big feet. She must take after you, Dani."

Waxing Gibbous

It's kind of crazy, honestly, how little the pregnancy actually affects me. I mean, sure, I have to pee all the time now, and the heartburn is so real, but everything else? Everything else is the exact same. Shelby is still her boundary pushing, outgoing self. Jeremiah is still reserved and strong. And for the most part, I'm still invisible. It turns out, no one at school really cares, now that I've come out and said it. My pregnancy has become a non-issue.

That is until I miss Jeremiah's Tae Kwon Do tournament.

Pregnancy brain is impossible. That's my excuse. I realize my mistake about eleven in the morning, which is of course, two hours into a three-hour event, so even if I did manage to convince my mom to drive me over there, I would only arrive in time to see the award ceremony.

Instead, I spend the time practicing what I'll say to Jeremiah.

Pregnancy brain. I forgot, and I'm sorry.

Sure enough, my phone rings at five past noon.

"Hey!" I answer with way too much forced cheer.

"I got first place in weapon forms." He doesn't even bother to say hi to me. I try to keep it light. "That's awesome. Good job!"

"Thanks," he says dryly, "it would have been nice if my girlfriend could have been there to see it."

Groan, there it is. "Yeah, I am so sorry. I overslept, and then I just… well this pregnancy, you wouldn't even believe, my brain is a million different places."

"Yeah. It seems like pregnancy is your go-to excuse for a lot of things these days."

"What's that supposed to mean?"

"Nothing."

"It sure didn't sound like nothing." I grit my teeth. "Jeremiah, I've been coming to your Tae Kwon Do tournaments for months, and this is the first time I've ever missed one. Can't you give me a break?"

He pauses for a few seconds before answering. "It's just really important to me, that's all."

I have to actually take the phone away from my ear while I process that. That I can't even be forgiven this one transgression. I steel my voice, then bring the phone back to my ear. "I asked you to come to one doctor's visit with me. One. So you could see our baby. *That* was important to me. But you couldn't do that."

I hang up the phone before he has a chance to respond. Part of me hopes he'll call me back, but he doesn't.

Last Quarter

At school on Monday, Jeremiah is in a much better mood. He walks with me to every single class, holds my books, does all the normal boyfriend things that I got so used to last year. The arm around the shoulders, the kisses before dropping me off at my classes. At the end of the day, he drives me home and comes inside with me. It's almost like how we used to be, before all of this mess, except I'm still pretty angry with him about our fight.

And he knows it, because as soon as we're alone in the house, he pulls me close. "Hey, I'm sorry, Dani."

"I know."

"How long are you gonna be mad at me?"

I close my eyes and count to ten. When I open them, I'm relaxed enough to speak. "I'm not mad anymore." And I'm not, not really. Disappointed, maybe. But not mad.

I reach down and grab his hand, placing it on my stomach. "I just want you to love her, like I do."

"I do," he says. But I can tell he's not sure, and I'm trying to understand. I am. But it's hard. Because for me, the baby is a part of me. For him, I guess it's just something that's happening around him. Like, he still isn't sure it's real. That's why I wanted him at the ultrasound, so he could see what I saw.

I don't know how to say that to him without starting the fight all over again, and I don't want to do that. Instead, I nod and let him off the hook.

He leans down and kisses me. "I'll be there next time, Dani. Anytime you need me. You name it, and I'll be there."

I smile. "Okay."

Jeremiah hangs around for dinner, trying to prove he's still a perfect boyfriend. He chats with my mom over homemade chicken parmesan and tossed salad. Of course, he's talking about school and college applications and Tae Kwon Do, and all the things that are important to him.

"Anyway, I finally sent my application to MIT in a few weeks ago," he says.

Mom raises her eyebrows. "That sounds wonderful."

It doesn't sound wonderful at all to me. "You're still planning on going to Boston?" I ask. "Even with a baby on the way?"

I have completely forgotten my resolve not to fight.

"Well, Dani, c'mon. I can't just put my life on hold."

"Why not?" I demand. "I am."

He ducks his head. "Maybe I should go."

Mom tries to keep him back with a reminder about the homemade cookies on the counter, but he's already standing up and heading out the door.

"You really should try not to argue with him so much," she says.

I shrug and make my way to the plate of cookies, grabbing a handful. "Why not?"

"Because, you're tethered to each other for life," she says. "Even if you don't stay together, you still have this baby. You still need a good relationship, so the baby doesn't suffer."

"Like you and Dad?" I ask. "You two don't get along."

"And wouldn't it be nicer for you if we did?"

I scowl. Of course it would, but it doesn't matter. I'm used to things. And it's silly to be fighting over this. Jeremiah and I may be going through a rough patch right now, but we'll get through it. Once he sees this baby, he won't want to leave her. He'll stay for her, and for me.

I take a bite of cookie under Mom's judgmental eye.

"You need to watch how much sugar you're eating," she says as I chew through the chocolatey goodness. "You're eating for two, you know."

"Do you have to say things like that, Mom?" I groan, "you sound like you stepped right out of a parenting book."

She raises an eyebrow. "Well the parenting books wouldn't have written it if it wasn't true. What you eat, the baby eats."

"And the baby loves chocolate chip cookies." I stuff the rest of the cookie in my mouth. "Mmmm, delicious." Crumbs spew from my mouth as I talk.

"Cute."

I swallow the monstrous bite. "Sorry."

After dinner, Mom and I settle on the couch to watch TV and work on our knitting. Hers is going, of course, a thousand times better than mine. She's about halfway done, and she's not just doing straight knitting like me. She has a pattern going of crisscross stitches and waves. It's actually really cool.

My project, on the other hand, is a lumpy grey mess, and I wish I'd never shown it to Jeremiah. He's so excited about it, a real homemade scarf from his girlfriend. Except, at the rate I'm going, he won't have it until he's twenty-five.

I stitch my way through two rows before giving up and putting it down. The stupid knitting needle keeps bumping into my stomach every time I try to lift off a stitch. Every time it does, Mom glances over and says, "slide it off gently, don't yank" which is almost worse than her nagging me about eating cookies.

I toss the knitting back in the bag and pick up my phone to play random games, but none of them really hold my interest. Then it happens.

Something moves.

I drop my hand to my stomach and wrinkle my eyebrow.

"Are you okay?" Mom asks from across the room.

"Yeah, I just felt something."

"Did the baby kick?"

"I don't know." It sounds like a stupid thing to say, but it's the truth. I'm really not sure. I feel it again. Like a fluttering, not even really like a strong kick. Not like in the movies, where women say they can feel the baby dancing around on their ribcage or whatever.

"Well, what's it feel like?"

"Like I've swallowed a live fish, and it's swimming around inside my guts."

She laughs. "Okay, yeah. That's probably the baby."

"It's weird."

"It gets weirder," she says, throwing on an additional stitch and looping her yarn around. "You'll see."

Waxing Gibbous

Mr. Craig holds me back after class again, and he has my Creative Writing journal in his hand, which can only mean one thing.

"Have you given any thought to the Poetry Slam next month?" he asks.

"I dunno," I say, rubbing my belly. "I've been a little preoccupied, you know?"

He nods. "You know life doesn't end just because you're having a baby, right?"

I guess. Sure seems like it has. Not that I had much of a life in the first place, but I have even less now. I've been fighting with Jeremiah more than ever, and I can't remember the last time Shelby and I had a girl's night.

He opens my notebook. "You've grown a lot this year, Danielle."

I snort. "No kidding." I'm bigger than ever.

Mr. Craig smiles indulgently. "Not like that. I mean your writing has evolved. Your voice is strong." He keeps flipping through pages until he stops on a poem I wrote three weeks ago about my mom. "This one. I think you should read this one at the Slam."

"No way," I say, "My mom wouldn't like it." He tilts his head and I keep explaining. "We're finally getting along for the first time and I don't think I can mess with that, you know?"

"You're finally getting along," he says, still watching me in that creepy teacher way that he has, "but does it count if you can't even tell her the truth about how you feel?"

Then he reads from the page. "*I can never compete with the ghost in your head.* That's powerful stuff, Dani. I think she deserves to hear your truth."

I'm not so sure. This sounds like a huge step backward with my mom, but he has a point. How can I say we're closer than ever when she doesn't know how I feel? I take the notebook out of his hand and read through the poem. "I'll think about it, okay?"

He nods. "Don't be afraid of your voice. It's strong, and it's important. I think the world would be a better place if you spoke up a little more."

I bite back a smile. "Thanks, I guess."

* * *

Jeremiah hasn't mentioned MIT or Boston at all for a couple weeks, so I guess I kind of hoped he had forgotten entirely about it or at least decided to stay closer to home. Wishful thinking, because he stops at my locker after school. "Dani, can we talk?"

Why wouldn't we be able to talk? Sometimes it feels like we never talk anymore. "Sure," I say, following him to his car. "What's up?"

He slides his hand into mine. "Look, you know I love you."

"Yeah..." No good conversation has ever started this way.

"And I really want to be there for you, with everything that's going on..."

Oh my god, he is breaking up with me.

"But..." I press.

He sighs. "But, I got accepted to MIT."

I stop walking. "You have got to be kidding me."

"I'm sorry, but it's really good opportunity."

I grit my teeth. "As good an opportunity as being a father to your child?" It's a passive-aggressive thing to say, I know, but I can't help it.

"I'll still be around for the baby."

"Really?" I snap, "You're going to drive down from Boston every night so you can help with the feedings and change some diapers?"

"Well, no, not every night..." his voice trails off.

I shake my head and storm away. This is all his mom's fault. I could tell when we told our parents, she was not going to let her precious oldest child's life get ruined just because his dumb girlfriend got pregnant. As if he didn't have his part to play in it all.

Jeremiah catches up with me. "Hey, why are you mad?"

"You're joking, right?" I yank my arm away. "You're leaving, Jer! In case you don't remember, you're half responsible for this!" I point to my stomach. "It's not just my problem. You were there. You made the same exact choices as I did! Why do you get to run away from this?"

"I'm not running away!"

"Yes, you ARE!" I scream, drawing the attention of everyone else in the parking lot.

I can't be around Jeremiah anymore right now. I'm not exactly fast, what with the pregnancy and all, but Jeremiah must have gotten the hint not to follow me, because I manage to lose him in a matter of seconds. Of course, now I'm halfway down the street in front of our high school without a ride home. Ugh.

I pull out my phone and dial Shelby's number.

At first, I'm afraid she's not going to answer, but she does. And she sounds breathless. "Hey," she pants, "what's up?"

"I need a ride home."

"Where's Jeremiah?"

"We had a fight."

"Oh…"

I listen for a while, waiting for her to say something else. Instead, I get treated to a faint suction sound, and Shelby starts giggling.

I wrinkle my nose. "Are you with Miles?"

She laughs. "Not exactly…"

"Some other boy?"

"You know Lucas, from our homeroom?" she asks, "He is…" more giggles, "an amazing kisser."

"Ew, Shelby, why did you answer the phone?" And more importantly, why am I still talking on it? I hang up, then lean against the nearest lamppost to weigh my options.

Option 1: Call Jeremiah and apologize, then beg him for a ride home. Nope. Not gonna happen. He's in the wrong here. He's choosing school over me, over our baby. He could go to UNC and get just as good an education and still be home every weekend to spend time with his daughter. But he's not.

Option 2: Walk home. Ugh. It's January, and I live all the way on the other side of town. The baby sits like a rock in my belly. I can't imagine lugging it all the way home.

Option 3… Call Mom.

I sigh, I don't have a choice.

Waxing Gibbous

For Valentine's Day, Jeremiah takes me to my favorite restaurant. He spent all morning apologizing for acting like a jerk, but that doesn't change the fact that he's leaving the state in six months. Taking me to Flannigan's Fish Fry is a good start though. It's where we ate on our first date, that Homecoming dance seems like an entire lifetime ago. It's a seafood place in the next town over that has the best crab cakes in the world. I'm not even joking. I don't think even Mom could make them that good. Plus, Mom has been not-so-subtly avoiding making any seafood for the past several weeks, because of mercury deposits and all that stuff. When I told her where we were going for our date, she spent half an hour online researching which fish are more likely to accumulate heavy metals and which aren't. Then she printed off a list of "safe fish" to eat.

I'm getting the crab cakes. End of story.

I go through about four different outfits before settling on the one I end up wearing. Trying to dress up while pregnant is a total joke. Because no matter what I put on, I still look pregnant.

I end up in a deep red sweater that comes down to my hips and some black leggings. Not exactly the picture of desire, but better than nothing. And Mom helps me curl my hair, so I end up looking pretty darn cute, not to sound like I'm bragging or anything.

Good enough to make Jeremiah step back and give me a good look over before stepping in the door. "You look nice."

"Thanks." I push some hair behind my ear. "You do too." Which is a lie, because Jeremiah is wearing literally the exact same outfit he wore to school.

It's not bad, it's just a polo and a pair of jeans. Nothing special. The only difference is, he threw some gel into his hair so it's a little spikier than usual.

He waves to my mom and promises to have me home before curfew before holding out his arm, real old-fashioned, and leading me out to his car.

It takes thirty minutes to drive to Flannigan's and we barely talk the entire drive over. We're both still smarting over the fight. I want to fix it, but I have no idea how. Because either way I spin it, we're both disappointing the other person.

I shift in the car seat and rub my hand over my stomach. The baby is sleeping. She's still and quiet like us.

At the restaurant, we at least have the food to talk about. But even that feels forced.

"You getting the crab cakes?" Jer asks. He knows me too well.

"Yeah, how about you?"

"Uh…" His eyes skim over the menu. "I'll probably just have the tilapia."

Tilapia, incidentally, is not one of the safe fish to eat while pregnant. I hate that I know that.

I nod. "Sounds good." We both fold our menu and set them on the table. I tap the corner of mine with my fingernail, trying to think of something to say. Jer looks just as uncomfortable.

"So," I begin, but at the same time Jeremiah starts to speak and we both break off at the same time.

"You go ahead," he says.

I look down. "It's not important."

"Oh."

Back to silence. This is awkward. This is like being on a first date all over again. I try again. "I think Shelby broke up with Miles."

Jeremiah shakes his head. "No she didn't."

"She was with some guy from our homeroom the other day," I argue.

"That's just Shelby, you know how she is."

I guess he's right. Shelby has always played it a little loose with the rules of monogamy, and Miles doesn't seem to care. It works for them, I suppose. It would drive me insane, if I were in his shoes though.

Jeremiah sips his water. "I don't get why you're even friends with her."

"She's funny."

"She's rude." He shakes his head. "She doesn't respect anyone."

"That's not true." I can feel another fight brewing, and I'm just not in the mood.

Luckily Jer isn't either. He just shrugs and says, "whatever."

We don't have to wait long before the waitress comes over. She's one of those overly familiar types who probably thinks that involving herself in every aspect of her customers' lives means she'll rake in the tips. Or maybe I'm just being exceptionally moody because I'm starving and not getting along well with my boyfriend on Valentine's Day, but she immediately grates on my nerves.

It doesn't help that I have a gigantic conversation starter attached to my stomach. And she notices it right away.

"Oh, out for one last romantic evening before the little one comes?" she coos.

I glance at Jeremiah, and his lip twitches slightly.

"Yeah, I guess," I say.

"So, what are we having to drink tonight?" She can't stop grinning at me. Jer sets down his menu. "Just water for me."

"Same," I put in.

He keeps on ordering. "And can I get the tilapia?"

"Sure thing," the waitress says. She clicks her pen and jots down his order. "And for you, honey?"

Nails on chalkboard. I hate pet names.

"The crab cakes," I say.

"The half order or full?"

"Full," I respond immediately.

She gets a glint in her eye. "Eating for two!"

Which makes that twice I've heard that particular phrase in the past two hours, two times more than necessary, in my opinion. Eating for two means that this date that I'm on with Jeremiah isn't just between him and me. It's between all three of us. I start to wonder if I'll ever get a chance to be truly alone anymore.

The waitress snaps her book shut and reaches down the take the menus from Jeremiah. "You two just enjoy your evening together. Once that baby comes, he'll have the run of the house. You'll be missing these date nights. Just you wait and see."

As she leaves, I let out a big sigh and turn to Jeremiah. "She thinks we're married."

"Or at least living together."

I look down. "No one expects the pregnant girl at the nice restaurant to be a sixteen-year-old loser, I guess."

"You're not a loser, Dani," Jer says, but I look away. Saying it doesn't change how I feel.

The waitress returns with two glasses of ice water, setting them on the table with a basket of doughy rolls. I snatch one up as soon as she leaves and start pulling it apart, releasing yeasty steam. While I chew my first bite, I mull over what she said, about the baby running the household. I'm not stupid. I know that having a baby is hard, and that it involves night time feedings and changing diapers and very little sleep and all. But I guess, in my mind, I always pictured doing those things with Jeremiah.

But Jeremiah doesn't live with me. So how is he going to help me with this baby?

I glance up, and he's looking at me with a worried expression. "What's up?"

"How are we going to do this?"

"Do what?"

"This, Jer, this!" I point at my bump. "How are we going to do this?"

But he doesn't know. He clearly doesn't know. He flounders for an answer, while we wait for our food. A stream of "um's" and "Well, I thought's" and I realize for the first time since I got pregnant that I'm doing all of this alone.

Completely alone. And I don't know why it took me so long to realize it, but now that I do, I feel so foolish. Jeremiah made his choice. He chose MIT over me, over the baby.

But I'm not even mad. Not anymore. Because a part of me always knew that he was going to make that choice. Part of me expected it. And another part of me knows that it was unfair of me to put him in that position in the first place.

By the time the plate of crab cakes is set in front of me, I've completely lost my appetite. I pick my way through one cake, then save the rest for a to-go container. Depressing, really, because everyone knows that reheated crab cakes aren't as good as the original thing.

On the drive home, I reach across the arm rest and slide my hand into Jeremiah's. I need him to know that I still want us to be a team, to be in this together. That even if he is going to school somewhere else, I still want him to come home to me and to our daughter.

Full Moon

Bowling nights were disbanded weeks ago, but after Christmas, Dad decided on a new father-daughter bonding ritual, and this is one I can actually get behind. Driving lessons.

Mom was a nervous wreck every time I sat behind the wheel, but Dad is completely ambivalent about the whole thing. He picks me up from school, hops out of his car and I slide into the driver's seat. Or more often than not these days, plop into the driver's seat. Then it's the open road for Dani Miller and her dad. No Ashley here. Even she can't think of a good excuse to insert herself into driving lessons.

It's kind of perfect. Without Ashley, I feel like I can actually talk to Dad. He's not the guy who cheated on my mom and is engaged to someone way too young for him anymore. He's just a normal dad.

And since it's the only thing I can think about these days, Jeremiah's decision to abandon me for MIT dominates the conversation as I drive out to Dad's favorite burger joint in the next town over.

"Well, Dani, you have to understand, he's got to make the choice that's best for him."

I hit the brakes a bit too hard as I pull into a parking spot. "Isn't being here for his kid best for him?"

He frowns, and I realize we're treading on dangerous territory.

Time to salvage the moment. "I mean, you could have moved across country too, but you stayed in town for me, right?"

"Yes," Dad says, "but that was different."

"How?"

"Well, I had already gone to college, established a career." He holds out his hand for his keys, then climbs out of the car. "Jeremiah is still young, and you aren't married."

Yet, I think, but I'm not stupid enough to say it aloud.

"He deserves a chance to make his own way in the world," Dad finishes as he opens the door for me.

I don't go in. "But what about me?"

"What about you?"

"Don't I deserve the same chances?"

"Of course you do, Dani."

I fold my arms and glare at the sidewalk. "But I won't get those chances, because of this baby. It's going to be like a thousand times harder for me. Just because I'm the girl and he's the boy, that means he gets to leave? That's not fair."

Hard not to imagine this conversation is about Dad. His jaw sets as he nods. "No, it's not fair. But you'll have your mom and me and even Ashley to help. So it's not a hopeless case either."

Great. Just what I need, Ashley's help with raising my baby.

If Dad's words couldn't appease me, at least bacon cheeseburgers and steak fries can. I know Mom would lose it if she knew what I was eating, but a girl can't survive on kale and brown rice for nine months. No matter how good it is for the baby. I need the grease and the salt and the chocolate mint milkshake on the side. Say what you will for divorced parents, at least Dad knows how to spoil me.

The baby is kicking up a storm by the time dinner's over. She definitely approves of chocolate mint milkshakes, and I rub my belly in an attempt to convince her to settle down.

"So," Dad says, "ready to head home?"

"Um, actually I have a question for you."

He raises an eyebrow. "Oh really?"

I fidget with my napkin. "Um, so the week after Spring Break, our school is doing a Poetry Slam. It's on Friday Night. Anyway, I was thinking I might be in it. And if you weren't too busy, maybe you could come?"

"Of course I'll be there, baby. You know I wouldn't miss it." He pulls out his cell to check dates. "When did you say it was?"

"March 22."

His face falls. "Oh."

"Oh, what?"

"Ashley and I booked a cruise for that week. We'll be gone until the next Wednesday."

I stare out of the corner of my eye at the happy family of four in the booth next to ours, my heart burning with jealousy. Maybe once, a long time ago, my family was that happy, but I don't remember it. All I remember is this.

"I'm really sorry, Dani-lion."

"I don't like it when you call me that," I snap, surprising even myself with my tone.

His eyebrows crinkle with confusing, and maybe a little hurt. "I'm sorry. I didn't know."

"It doesn't matter," I say, refusing to look at him as I push my plate away and start gathering my jacket and purse. "Can we just go home?"

"If that's what you want, sure."

I push my way through the crowd back to the parking lot, Dad a few steps behind me. As we approach the car, I turn and hold out my hand, expecting him to hand me the keys, but he doesn't. Without a word, he sits in the driver's spot, and just like that, I'm back in the passenger seat.

Waning Gibbous

Mom wasn't joking when she said the movements get weirder. I'm pretty sure this baby is training to be a dancer or something, the way she's always kicking and jumping and stuff. I've started to notice she's most active when I'm eating, flopping around like a fish. She must like Mom's cooking.

Lunch is one of the few times Jeremiah is actually interested in the baby. He usually sits right next to me, and as soon as I feel the baby kicking, I give him a nudge with my elbow, and he reaches over to feel. I mean, it's hard not to get excited about it.

Except every once in a while, when Jeremiah and I do our little ritual of feeling tiny baby kicks, I catch Shelby giving us a sarcastic look like she thinks we're being ridiculous. She doesn't get it. How could she? It's not like she's ever been pregnant before.

Whenever I offer to let her feel, she just shakes her head and says she's not interested, so I've stopped offering.

Usually, by the evening, the baby has calmed down, so Mom hasn't gotten to feel a kick yet. I can tell it's bugging her, that the baby is most active during the day. To the point where I wonder if she thinks I'm doing it on purpose. Except, that's crazy. How could I possibly control that? It's just bad luck.

Mom lucks out today, because the baby has decided to practice all of her favorite moves right as Mom gets home from work. I'm lying on my side on the sofa, trying to ignore the rhythmic beat on my lower abdomen and reading my History textbook, when Mom walks in.

"Hey baby, how you doing?"

"Good," I groan. "I guess. The baby won't stop kicking. She's driving me insane."

Mom pauses on her way to the kitchen, then turns back to me. "She's kicking right now?"

"Yeah, hasn't stopped since Jer dropped me off."

"Can I feel?"

I look up from my textbook. Mom has this look on her face. It's hard to describe. Like she's looking at a ghost. I nod. "Yeah, of course."

She drops her purse on the end table and kneels on the floor next to the sofa, then places a hand on my stomach.

"Not there," I say, pointing to a spot just under my ribs. "She's up here."

"Oh." Mom slides her hand to where I pointed, waits a few seconds. Then the baby kicks. Thump, thump, thump, in quick succession.

"Did you feel it?" I ask.

Mom's mouth widens into a faint smile, and she closes her eyes. "Yes."

She doesn't remove her hand, like I expect her to. She just kind of sits there, feeling the little vibrating thumps on my stomach, her eyes still closed.

"Mom?" I whisper. This is getting weird.

She draws in a long low breath, then turns toward my stomach and kisses the spot where the little foot was pounding. Then she stands up and kisses me right on the forehead before heading to the kitchen to make dinner.

Definitely weird.

Last Quarter

Fun fact about pregnancy, there are so many tests. I pee in a cup literally every single time I go to Dr. Henderson's office. My aim has improved significantly since that horrible visit to the women's health clinic four months ago. I'm used to all the normal things like blood pressure and heart rate, but I hate the blood draws. And this week, I get the most important one.

At least that's what my mom would have me think.

Gestational diabetes. Apparently sometimes the mere act of being pregnant messes up the way some you process sugar, which can be really dangerous. So the way they test it is they make you drink this disgusting sugar drink then not eat or drink anything for an hour, then have your blood drawn to see how much sugar is in it.

No one told me I was going to have my blood drawn a second time. I spend all morning having nervous flashbacks to the first blood draw. Which isn't helped at all by Mom's near constant nagging every time she sees me eat a piece of candy.

I can't help it. The baby has cravings.

And right now, she's craving Sour Patch Kids. What am I supposed to do, ignore her?

Mom is watching my Sour Patch Kids consumption like she's getting paid to do it. Every time one of those delicious gummy candies pops into my mouth, she sighs. Loudly. After five, she says, "maybe you should slow down, Dani."

After ten, she says, "That's probably enough."

If I keep going after that… "Gestational diabetes is a real thing, Dani. You could end up on bedrest. You could end up delivering early. Your baby could get sick."

"I know, Mom!" I want to keep eating, but with each new reprimand, the candy loses a little of its flavor.

She cuts me off completely after lunch. She has her phone open next to her, with the timer counting down to the exact second until I have to drink the Kool-aid. Not real Kool-aid, obviously, but the sugary concoction the doctor gave me at the last visit. I got to pick between orange and grape. Quite frankly, they both sounded awful, but I chose grape.

Now, as I'm staring at the bottle, I'm having my doubts about the wisdom of my choice.

Mom watches her phone, and when the last second counts down, and it reads 3:15, she looks up at me. "Go."

I open the bottle and chug. I have to get it down fast. That's the rule. Don't ask me to explain why. Something to do with the amount of sugar in it. I'm just doing what Dr. Henderson told me to do, because according to her, if I mess this up, I have to do it again. And I'm not in the mood for another needle poke if I can avoid it.

When I finish, I slam the empty bottle back on the counter. "Done."

Mom writes down the time on a sticky note. "Okay. We'll head up to the doctor's office in about thirty minutes. Make sure you're ready to go."

I slide off the stool. "Great." Thirty minutes. Just enough time to zone out in front of the TV.

I've just about fallen asleep on the sofa, when Mom shakes my shoulder. "Time to go, Dani."

Urgh. I struggle to sit up. I've officially reached the point in the pregnancy when I'm starting to feel clumsy. Some of those things I used to take for granted are now way more difficult than they have any right to be.

Like tying shoes. Who knew tying shoes could be such a chore? I didn't. I've completely switched to slip on everything at this point. I yank on a pair of ankle boots and stand. "Alright, let's do this."

I must look white, because Mom hands me my jacket with a gentle reminder. "It's just a little poke. Don't look at the needle."

"Why did you have to remind me there'd be a needle?" I groan.

"Ha ha ha," she jibes, "Come on."

Mom tries to keep my mind off of the impending doom while we drive. "Have you thought about names?" she asks.

"Um, a little."

"And…?"

"I was thinking I might name her after Granny?"

Mom's face is completely blank as she turns onto the next street. "That's nice."

"Well," I continue, "because she's been such an important part of my life."

"Yes."

"I just thought it'd be a nice legacy or something."

"What does Jeremiah think about the name Evelyn?"

"I dunno."

We're entering dangerous territory. Jeremiah and I haven't been in sync with each other for a while. I feel like we both are angry at the other for something, but I don't know what. I just know that we sit in silence more often than not these days. I used to feel like I could talk to him about anything. But now, I feel like every time I open my mouth, I risk starting another fight. And I don't want to fight anymore.

I expect Mom to press the issue, but she doesn't. Thankfully.

When we get to Dr. Henderson's office, the receptionist asks a bunch of questions about when I drank the grape drink, how long it took me to drink it. Have I eaten or drunk anything since? Mom has all the answers, so I don't have to worry about it. I just stand there silently, awaiting my fate.

The receptionist leans over to the buzzer. "We have a blood draw. Needs to be done in seven minutes." Then she turns back to me. "You can leave your sample now."

Oh joy.

I'm way too nervous about the blood test to pee in a cup, and I miss and splash urine all over the place. Oh well. They'll just have to deal with it. Then I go back to the waiting room to fidget nervously for the remaining five minutes until I get stabbed with the needle again.

Yuck.

Mom's no help. She just sits there knitting away at another baby blanket. A second one. One isn't enough, apparently. This one is yellow and pink. My daughter's going to grow up thinking she's a princess or something. When she notices me fidgeting, she lays a hand on my knee. "Calm down, Dani."

"I don't like needles."

"I know, but you need to calm down. Think of something else. Something pleasant."

Like what? My big old pregnant belly? The stretch marks I noticed last night as I was going to bed? My boyfriend who won't talk to me? My best friend who no longer returns my phone calls? There's nothing pleasant in my life right now. But I can't talk to Mom about that kind of stuff, so instead I just shrug. "Whatever."

The nurse calls my name to go on back, and I stand, casting a glance back at my mom.

"I'll be right here, if you need me."

"Thanks."

I follow the nurse back to the phlebotomy station. That's a new word I learned, thanks to this awesome pregnancy. Phlebotomists draw blood. I can't imagine a worse job to have. I'd take filing paperwork over that any day.

I sit in the chair and prop my arm up on the rest, then turn my face away. Mom's advice might be good. Just don't look at it. The phlebotomist is a twenty-something geeked-out girl with curly hair that reminds me a little of Shelby's, except it's light brown instead of black. I'm not looking at her, though. I'm looking at the cat calendar she has hanging over her computer. Cats.

She's a crazy cat lady. I'm getting my blood drawn by a crazy cat lady. What's worse, the more I look around the room, the more evidence I have that she has way too many cats at home. There are pictures of cats stuck to the wall behind her computer, and there's a frame that says, "We heart Mommy," only inside of the frame, instead of pictures of children, she has two cats. One is solid black, the other solid white.

"Okay!" she says. Her voice is high pitched. "All done!"

"Really?" I look down. Sure enough. I've got a bandage on the crook of my elbow, and she's pulling the elastic tourniquet off my arm.

"Yup, easy peasy!" She slides the tray of blood vials into a fridge and then pulls her gloves off.

"I didn't even feel it."

"That means I did a good job!" she says with a smile.

She's way too happy about this. I slide off the chair. "So, what are your cats' names?"

"Chloe and Zoe."

"Those are nice names." Names I definitely cannot use for my baby now. I can't imagine having to tell my child she was named after a cat.

"Thanks." She points to the door. "You're in exam room four."

I nod and head on down.

* * *

Negative. The test for gestational diabetes comes back negative, and I can't stop myself from gloating. "See, Mom," I tease as I grab a brownie out of the pan on the counter. "You were worried over nothing."

"It's not a free for all, Dani. Just because you don't have diabetes, that doesn't mean you can eat anything you want."

I roll my eyes. "I know, but it's nice to know I can indulge a little, right?" I take a bite of the brownie and actually moan with pleasure. It's so good. Too bad the Booster Club kicked Mom out, because they are missing out on some seriously good snacks.

I eyeball the pan, thinking I might grab another, but Mom stops me. She snaps the lid back on. "Save room for dinner."

"You know," I tease, "if you didn't want me to eat them, you shouldn't have made them."

She gives me a look. The suggestion that my mom should stop baking is kind of like suggesting the world should stop turning on its axis.

"Okay, okay," I mutter, stuffing the last bite in my mouth. "I'll slow down."

I swallow the bite and wipe my mouth with a napkin. "Can Jeremiah come over tonight?"

She frowns. "I have an HOA meeting tonight."

I know. That's why I'm asking. I figure, maybe if Jeremiah and I have a little alone time, a little romance, maybe even a little… maybe we wouldn't fight so much.

"We'll just work on our homework, I promise." I rub my belly absentmindedly.

She turns away to chop vegetables at the counter, so I don't have to watch her debate, then eventually nods. "Okay, fine."

"Thanks!" I say, waddling up to my bedroom so I can tell him the good news.

* * *

I meet Jeremiah at the front door, not even bothering to let him in before throwing my arms around him and kissing him. Hard.

His hands find my waist and pull me away. "Whoa, Dani, what's gotten into you?"

"Hormones, mostly." They are raging. I go from normal to weepy in seconds flat. But mostly, I feel sexy. And it has been forever since Jeremiah and I have had any real alone time.

Surely, he wants it too.

I pull him through the door and toward the stairs to my room. "Mom won't be back until nine. It's just you and me."

He grins in spite of himself. "Okay then."

At first, everything seems fine, but as things start to heat up, my stupid belly keeps getting in the way. Jeremiah rolls onto me without thinking and I whimper in pain, sending him scurrying across the bed.

"Side by side?" I suggest, but everything feels awkward, like our bodies just don't fit together like they used to.

"Maybe if you're on top," he says, but as soon as I climb over him, he gets uncomfortable, his hands searching for anywhere to hold that isn't completely changed by my huge stomach.

"This isn't working."

I hate to admit it, but he's right. All of my raging hormones have left the building. I groan and sit at the edge of the bed, my back to him.

He creeps up beside me, his hand on my back. "Hey, Dani, it's okay."

"No it's not!" I can feel weepy hormones creeping in, and I will do anything to avoid crying over something this silly. "I just want to feel close to you again."

"Again?"

"Like at Langley beach last fall," I explain. "I just felt so… I don't know."

"Connected," he finishes.

"Yeah."

He kisses my cheek. "We're still connected, Dani. We'll always be connected."

Sure, because of this baby. This baby which is changing everything.

New Moon

"So," Shelby says as she plops into the chair next to me during Homeroom. "What's going on with you and Jeremiah?"

I lean back as far as I can in these stupid plastic seats. Pregnancy and high school desks do not mix, and there's hardly any room for me to stretch out. Lately, it seems the baby has decided to take up residence in my ribcage, and it hurts.

I push on my bump to try to convince the baby to move. "What do you mean?"

"You guys are just acting weird. Like, you used to be all over each other. Always holding hands and stuff. Now you're being totally cold around each other. It's weird."

I sigh. I should have expected her to notice.

"I don't know," I say, "things are just kind of rough lately. We had another fight last week." The baby lands a hard kick to my ribs and I cringe.

"What about?" Shelby leans toward me, all ears.

I glance at her, debating. The fact is, Shelby and I haven't exactly been seeing eye to eye either. I'm not sure I really want to spill the beans about why Jer and I have been fighting. Then again... I can't exactly talk to anyone else.

I shift my desk closer to hers, so we can whisper. "So, Jer came over to my house. And we started... you know... fooling around. Nothing crazy. But I mean," I shrug, "we haven't exactly done anything in a while."

Shelby nods, knowingly. Then again, what would she know about it?

"Anyway," I continue, "the pregnancy hormones start kicking in, and I'm like… ready to go, then he just stops."

"*He* stopped?" She's positively flabbergasted.

"Yeah. Like, totally not interested."

"Wow," she snorts. "I have never had a guy quit on me."

I shift away. "Thanks, that makes me feel so much better."

But she's not done with me. She twirls a black curl around her finger. "Well what did he say?"

"Basically, that the pregnancy thing is a huge turn off."

Shelby shrugs. "Well, maybe it is?" But the way she says it makes me absolutely hate her. I just want to snap her little neck. Sex with Jeremiah isn't just sex. It's more than that. She doesn't understand. It's always been about loving each other. When he turns me down, it's not because I'm pregnant. It's because he doesn't love me anymore.

She's already sinking back into her seat, looking smug, and I wish I hadn't told her anything.

* * *

I catch up to Jeremiah before lunch. "Hey."

"Hey." He pecks me quickly on the cheek. "How's your day been?"

"Okay, I guess." I grab his hand. "Listen, can we talk?" I pull him out of the cafeteria doorway and away from the stream of hungry teenagers.

He gazes longingly at the coveted food, then turns his gaze back to me. "What's wrong?"

"About the other night…"

"Dani," he mumbles, casting his eyes around the hallway, as if anyone would know what we're talking about. "Here? Really?"

"I just feel…" I don't even know how to put words to this feeling. I look down at his hands in mine and trace circles on them with my thumb. "I love you. That hasn't changed for me."

He leans down until his forehead is resting against mine, and he slides his hands around my waist. "It hasn't changed for me either."

I sigh. "I just don't understand what happened. Am I just so gross and ugly now, you can't even imagine being with me?"

"No!"

"Because I'm the same me. I'm still Dani!"

He steps away, glancing around nervously. "Well, you are and you aren't."

"What's that supposed to mean?"

"You're preoccupied," he motions toward my stomach, "with the baby and all."

"Well, I mean. I should be, shouldn't I? Having a baby is a big deal."

"Exactly. And you just made that decision for the both of us."

My heart stops. How could he put that on me? "You told me to decide. You said it was my body, so it had to be my choice."

"Well, I thought you would decide to get rid of it!"

I pinch my eyes shut to try to keep from crying. "You forced me to make the decision by myself, so no matter what happened, it would be my fault. That wasn't fair."

"That's not what I did!"

"Yes, it is." I step away from him. "You checked out. I told you I was pregnant, and you checked out. You sat in the waiting room playing games on your phone while I was poked and prodded by some stranger."

"Dani..." he begins.

"I want us to be in this together, Jer." I reach up and kiss him lightly on the lips, but the very act feels so desperate and I hate myself for it. "I can't do this alone."

He hesitates. I swear, he hesitates. Then, he wraps his arms around my shoulders and pulls me close, hugging me tightly against his chest. "You're not alone."

Waxing Crescent

Maybe Jer's right. Maybe I am preoccupied. All I know is every time I'm with him, I start having big conversations. I can't help it. Mom says I'm nesting. Whatever that means.

"Preparing for the baby," she replies, "Making sure your home is in order, ready for her to come. Most women do it."

And she's right. Every chance I get, I'm in the baby's room, fixing it up. Mom and I found a ton of baby clothes cheap at a second-hand store, and I spend hours folding and refolding them. Dad, in a show of unexpected solidarity sprang for a crib and matching dresser. I think Ashley put him up to it. She's even trying to quit smoking, because she knows it's bad for the baby.

It's like Dad finally got it in his head that he's becoming a grandfather.

Now, Jeremiah on the other hand. I'm not sure he's ever really grasped the idea of being a dad. I think he's still kind of hoping that this is all some elaborate prank.

Hence, the big talks. I try to sneak the big talks in when we're in the middle of a romantic endeavor. Like, maybe he'll be more open to listening to me when his shirt is unbuttoned.

It's hit or miss.

It always starts the same. I kiss his ear and climb on his lap, then slide my hand along the back of his neck. "So, I was thinking," I say as he runs his hand over my stomach. "Maybe I could move up to Boston with you?"

He scoffs. "What?"

"We just never really talked about us, and the baby, and what we're going to do after she's born."

"What do you mean?"

He's actually going to make me say it. I can't believe it. "Well, are we planning on..." I squirm, nervously, "like living together or, I don't know..."

"Getting married?"

I shrug.

He squares his shoulders and leans his head back, so he's staring at the ceiling, not at me. "I mean, I guess I've thought about it."

"And...?"

"And, I think you should finish high school."

I nod and run my fingers through his hair. "I've been looking at online school. I just need to convince Mom to let me be homeschooled."

"Yeah, homeschooled." He puts the emphasis on the *home*. "Here, with your mom, so she can help you."

"Okay, but after that. After I graduate, what about then?"

"I don't know, Dani." He sits up and kisses me. "Let's just take it one step at a time. You're worrying too much."

It's not a complete lost cause. It's not a confirmation either. At least he still thinks of us as together. At least he still sees a future with me.

Waxing Gibbous

I am getting so sick of doctor's visits, probably because they take forever. Not the actual visit with the doctor, which takes like five minutes, but the sitting around in the waiting room, then the waiting around in the exam room. I'm so done.

Mom doesn't seem to mind. She just sits in the waiting room and knits the whole time. She has powered through the second baby blanket which—I have to admit—looks amazing. Now she's been working on little outfits, hats and matching booties. My baby is going to be decked out in knitwear for over a year. She's a woman obsessed. If anyone's nesting, it's her, not me.

Right now, she's sitting next to me working on knitting a stuffed rabbit, so the baby "has a friend." Her words, not mine.

I brought my laptop so I can work on my poem. Mr. Craig said it's good, but it needs a few tweaks to be amazing, and for the first time, I kind of want to be amazing.

Editing is the worst, because it largely involves reading the same words over and over again, just to make one tiny change. After about ten minutes of staring at the computer screen and only changing a few things around, I click save and shut the lid.

"What're you working on?" Mom asks without looking up.

"Um," I guess I should tell her about the Slam. "There's a big poetry thing at school next week."

"Poetry thing?" she repeats.

"Like a Poetry Slam. You stand up and read an original work." I push hair behind my ear. "It's not a big deal. You don't have to come or anything."

She lowers her knitting. "But I want to come!"

"Mom, it's really not a big deal."

"I think it's wonderful! You're joining something, you're getting involved. I want to support you."

Oh brother, not this again. "I'm not joining something, Mom. I'm just reading a poem." I mean, seriously. What would be the point of getting involved at school at this point?

I don't even know what I'm going to do next year, when I have a baby. I try to imagine me going to school full time, but I can't seem to make it work out in my head. Who would watch the baby?

I've been thinking a lot about what to do, and I'm still coming up with nothing. Last year, I was so sure I'd graduate, then go off to school with Jeremiah, but now, I'm not so sure. I'm starting to see why so many girls end up dropping out when they're pregnant. I know Mom would be disappointed though. Plus, I still want the option of going to college someday, even if I can't right away.

I've been trying to research my options in my spare time, and pretty much everything I've come up with is online school. North Carolina has an online K-12 program for homeschooled students. I think if I play my cards right, I might be able to convince Mom to let me switch. That way I can stay home with the baby all day and take classes on my own time. The only problem is, as she would say, I have a problem committing to something and sticking with it. A year ago, that might have been true, but now I just want high school to be over, and this seems like the fastest way to do it.

If I can convince Mom.

I doubt the Poetry Slam would help, but she's already got her mind set on coming, so I guess I have to go through with it. I sort of hoped if I waited until the last minute to tell her, she wouldn't be able to come, and would therefore miss out on hearing my poem.

Because who am I kidding? Mr. Craig may think I need to clear the air with my mom before this baby comes, but I know if she hears this poem, the air isn't going to get cleared. It'll just be a whole lot hazier.

It's too late to change it though. He's already submitted the poem to the theater teacher who runs the whole Slam, so if I try to back out now, or switch to something else, it'll mess up the program.

I have one week to get used to the idea that Mom is going to know how I actually feel.

Finally.

Full Moon

On the night of the Poetry Slam, Jeremiah is nowhere to be found. I've called his cell about a million times, and he's not picking up. I'm furious. And hurt. And not to mentioned humongous and uncomfortable.

Mom made me wear a dress and patent leather ballet flats so shiny I'm pretty sure Ray Charles could see me walking down the street. I tried to explain to her that poetry was an art form and I could get away with jeans and sneakers, but she said I'm performing so I have to look my best. I pace around backstage trying to concentrate on my poem, but inside I'm fuming that Jeremiah hasn't shown up yet. It's hard. I keep checking my phone to see if he's texted, and the whole time I'm thinking about how many Tae Kwon Do tournaments I've sat through, and just how boring those are, and how he *knows* I'm nervous about sharing my poetry, and yet he's still not here.

I try calling him again, only to get his voicemail. "Jer," I snap, "It's me. Dani. Where are you? I can't believe you've abandoned me here. Tonight." My voice cracks, and I take a deep breath. "I thought I could depend on you." As soon as I hang up, I worry I was too harsh, but oh well. It's too late now.

I turn off my phone, because the Poetry Slam is starting, and it's a strictly no phone zone for the next two hours. I'm slated pretty late in the program. Mr. Craig says I've got a strong voice, and it's important to end on the stronger pieces. People like to leave feeling something powerful.

Unfortunately, this gives me a lot of time to dwell. I pace around backstage and sip on a bottle of water, which is a horrible idea, because my bladder is tiny. I end up going to the bathroom three times before it's my turn. Even so, I still feel like I might pee in my leggings as I wait behind the curtain for

Mr. Craig to announce my name.

"And now, a promising voice from our junior class..." He glances to where I stand in the wings, giving me an encouraging smile before turning back to the microphone. "Danielle Miller."

The crowd goes silent, then a light smattering of applause. I step onto the stage, my stomach proceeding me. I can hear them whispering, all the parents of all my classmates. I don't need to be in the crowd to know what they're saying. Pregnant girl. What could she have to say?

I step up to the mic, then clear my throat. "The Perfect Daughter."

All my life, I've tried to be
The perfect daughter.
The one who is sweet and womanly,
Yet strong and determined.
The one she wants me to be.
But at every turn, I disappoint.
I fail to see
The pride I know my mother wants to feel,
But can't, because I'm not
Smart enough
Pretty enough
Happy enough
Involved enough
Friendly enough
Enough of anything.
Everything.
Not enough.
It started when I was born.
Or maybe nine months after.
When the one she loved left forever
And all that was left was me.
Second best in every way
It was evident in the way her eyes rolled over me
Lost focus.

Evident in the set of her lips when she looked at me,
But never really saw
The perfect daughter she longed for.
Evident that I could never live up to the ghost in her head
That she doesn't love me. Not like him.
Never like him.
And I will never be
The perfect daughter.

I fall silent and step away from the microphone. It takes every ounce of my energy to stay on that stage and watch the audience digest my words. Then the applause comes. Not tentative like before I started talking. Real applause.

I take a quick bow, then duck off the stage.

Mr. Craig gives me a quick side hug. "That was excellent, Danielle."

"Thanks," I say breathlessly. I'm still in shock. The Danielle Miller from August would never have stepped on that stage. "Is it okay if I go out to the audience to find my mom?"

Mr. Craig nods. "Of course."

"Great." I gather up my things, then look over my shoulder. "I'll see you, Monday."

He nods, then steps onto the stage to introduce the next poet.

* * *

I find Mom pacing in the front lobby. "Mom?" I ask as I lay a hand on her shoulder.

She pulls away, and when she turns around, I can see tears on her cheeks.

"We're going home," she snaps.

"Can't we talk?"

But she refuses to open up. "We'll talk when we get home."

I knew it. All that talk of Mr. Craig's. Let her hear my truth, but she can't take it. My truth is too much. All the exhilaration I felt on stage is gone, leaving me with a sinking feeling in my stomach that has nothing to do with the baby.

She doesn't waste a second. As soon as we walk through the front door, she lays into me.

"Do you even know how embarrassing that was for me? Listening to you rant about what a terrible mom I am?"

I open my mouth to argue, but she cuts me off.

"When I have worked so hard to put a roof over your head, to make sure you have nutritious meals to eat, every opportunity in the world. And you have to go and embarrass me in front of my friends? The other moms at your school? What were you thinking?"

"I didn't mean to embarrass you."

She scoffs. "Oh really? Haven't I always just been some burden on your life? Poor little Dani, too cool for her mom. Doesn't want to be seen with the crazy lady who bakes cookies and joins the Booster Club? Oh no. She's too good for that."

"Mom, no—" I begin, but she keeps going.

"You have no idea the sacrifices I've made for you! And you just throw them all away. You don't care about anything or anyone. You know nothing about what it means to be a good mother!"

"I just wanted…" I take a step toward her, but she's already turned and left the room. Her bedroom door slams, making me jump.

I can't hold the tears back, so I do the only thing I can think. I yank my phone out of my purse, turn it back on, and dial. Dad's out of town, so I have to try for Jeremiah. It rings several times, then goes to voicemail.

"Jeremiah?" I sob, "I need to see you. Please."

I pace around the living room, crying into my hand, then decide to try for the next best thing. Shelby. I call her, then sink onto the couch as I wait for her to pick up. Two rings, then straight to voicemail. Either her phone is off or she blocked my call.

I don't even bother leaving her a voicemail.

I can't sit still. My leg keeps shaking. I stand up, pace a lap around the room, then get frustrated and sit back down. This continues for about fifteen minutes until I grab my mom's keys off the kitchen counter and leave.

I don't even know where I'm going, I just know I need to think. I've ruined everything. All the progress I've made with Mom over the past few weeks. Gone. I'm terrified. And heartbroken. And the one person I want right now, my mom, isn't speaking to me.

I drive around aimlessly for a few minutes, then turn around and head to Jeremiah's house. He's not answering my phone calls, he didn't show up to the Poetry Slam, and I am pissed. All my worry about mom has turned into fury directed at him. He's got some answering up to do, and I'm just emotional enough to finally say what I've been feeling all year.

That this is all his fault.

He got me pregnant. Then he pressured me to get an abortion, even though he knew I wouldn't be able to. He's been pretending to want this baby with me, but he couldn't even show up for one measly ultrasound? He's supposed to be my partner. We said we'd love each other forever. Then he decides to go to school in a completely different state. So why all this distance? Why the avoidance?

I want answers.

I pull into his driveway and kill the engine. I'm so furious, I don't even notice his car is missing, so it's a pretty big surprise when his younger brother answers the door and unceremoniously tells me that "Jeremiah's not here."

"Well, do you know where he is?" I demand.

He shrugs.

"Great." I storm back to the car without another word. Where the hell is he? I hop back on the road and head to the nursing home. Granny has never failed to put my mind at ease. I need her calm, I need to find my own. But I can't. All I can think about is Mom and our fight. And Jeremiah being gone.

Unfortunately, when I get to the nursing home, I find out that Granny can't see anyone today. Minnie's gone and I don't recognize the woman behind the desk who tells me that Granny's having a hard day.

I'm on the verge of tears. "Can you tell her Dani's here?"

The nurse shakes her head sadly. "I'm afraid she won't understand."

I sink into the nearest waiting room chair and put my head in my hands. As well as I can at least with this awful belly in my way.

"Are you okay?" The nurse rests her hand on my shoulder.

"I'm fine," I say through my tears, "just leave me alone." Thankfully, she listens and walks away, but I can still feel her eyes watching me from the reception desk.

Everything is wrong. This was not how my junior year was supposed to go. I was supposed to be enjoying the last year with my boyfriend. I was supposed to be having fun with my friends, going to the movies, hanging out at the beach, enjoying life.

I was not supposed to get pregnant.

I can't go home, so I go to the only other place I can think of. Shelby's house.

It takes a while to get there, because she lives in the nice part of town. The houses are huge, and all painted varying shades of the same boring beige. McMansions. That's what Mom calls them. I can kind of see her point. They all look so… unnecessary. Unimportant.

I find her house and park the car. And that's when I see it. Jeremiah's car, I would recognize it anywhere, sitting in the driveway. Why is his car here?

Something is going on, I can feel it in my bones. Earth has stopped spinning on her axis, and I'm suddenly very aware of everything. The slick of last night's rain on the concrete, the cold harsh breeze that rustles through the trees and in my hair. I didn't put on a jacket when I left the house. I haven't needed one all winter, I've been so hot all the time.

Not now. Now I feel like ice and wind. I shiver as I climb the stairs. Whatever is behind that door, I know it's not going to be good. But I have to see.

* * *

I push the door open. "Shelby? Jer?" I call into the empty hallway. No reply. They're not in the front room, which makes perfect sense, because Shelby's parents are super strict about the baby grand piano in there. I tiptoe down the hallway and peer into the den. Still empty. So they're not hanging around watching TV or something. It's too cold to use the pool, which leaves only one place left to look.

My eyes drift upward, to the ceiling.

Shelby's bedroom.

I pinch my eyes closed and whisper a quick prayer. "Please, don't let them be doing what I think they're doing."

But I have to look. Just like driving past a car wreck, I know I'm not going to like what I see, but I have to know. I take my time climbing the stairs. No need to rush this. Shelby's room is at the end of the hallway, so I have a long time to contemplate what awaits me. But no amount of contemplation really prepares me for the actual sight.

I open the door slowly, quietly, and for a second, they don't even notice me. For a second, I'm just watching the two of them, seated on her bed, leaning into each other. Their lips locked. From this angle, the boy could be any boy. Brown hair and tan, but his shirt is off, and I could recognize those freckled shoulders anywhere.

He's not any boy.

He's Jeremiah. My Jeremiah.

"Oh my God," I whisper.

It would almost be funny, if it weren't so horrible. The way they scramble, the way Jeremiah pushes her away. They rush to pick up clothes. Her shirt, discarded on the floor, his hanging on the back of the chair. I don't see anymore, because I'm running for the stairs, taking them two at a time, my belly growing heavier with each step.

I can't do this. Not today, not right now. I can't see Jeremiah like that, and I definitely can't talk to him like this. At this point, my only goal is escape. When given the choice of fight or flight, I will run and hide every time. It's only natural.

I can't get the sight of Jeremiah and Shelby out of my head. Every time I blink, I see him kissing her, and I feel like I'm going to throw up.

I manage to make it down the stairs and out Shelby's front door before the tears start flowing.

Jeremiah.

My Jeremiah.

I can't even believe it. What is he doing with her? Shelby? He's always hated her, or at least pretended to. It was all a lie. The whole time. How long has this been going on? Would it feel like less of a betrayal if he were with a different girl? I think it would.

The door slams behind me, and I hurry down her front steps. I haven't really run in months, definitely never with this bowling ball attached to my stomach, and the steps are still slippery from last night's rain.

When I hit the third step, my foot slides out from beneath me, and I go down.

Full Moon

I wake up to the sight of Jeremiah leaning over me. "Dani? Dani?"

I try to sit up.

"Don't move," he orders, "I've called an ambulance."

"What happened?"

"You hit your head on the concrete." He kneels next to me and pushes hair out of my eyes, but I yank my face away.

"I want to go home." What home? I remember my fight with my mom and groan.

"You need to go to the hospital." He's pretty insistent. I want to tell him to go to Hell and never come back.

He must have read the thoughts on my face. "Dani, I'm sorry. It just happened."

"Leave me alone." I pull out of his grasp and start to stand, but my head is swimming, and I fall back on my bottom. I want to die. Crawl into a hole and die. Jeremiah rubs my back like some sort of good boyfriend and not the lying, cheating dirtbag that he is.

I hear the sirens before I see them, so I close my eyes and wait. Within a few minutes, the paramedics arrive. They flit around me, talking too fast and asking questions I don't know the answer to.

"She's pregnant," Jeremiah offers.

No shit, Sherlock. Even the paramedic gives him a look like he's some sort of idiot.

"How far along?"

"Uh…" Jeremiah looks nervously at me.

"Thirty-three weeks," I grumble. He should know. If I have to know, then so should he. The medics wrap a blood pressure cuff around my arm, then lift me onto a stretcher. All the while, Jeremiah and Shelby watch me like they actually care, which I know is a lie.

Jeremiah turns toward the house. "Let me go get my wallet. I'll ride with you." He must have taken it out of his pocket to fool around with my best friend.

"No, I don't want you there."

"But, the baby…" he looks back and forth from Shelby to me. Tough decision, I guess.

I make it easier for him. "Don't worry about the baby."

* * *

I'm not sure how long it takes to get me to the hospital. I'm not really paying attention. At some point, they stick an IV in me and hook up some fluid. Saline solution, I assume. I don't even feel the needle go in.

I don't care about anything, because all I can think about is Jeremiah. It feels like my heart has been shattered into a million different pieces. Suddenly I get what they mean when they say "heartbroken" because I'm about a thousand percent sure my heart won't be working properly for a long time. And it hurts. Like really, physically hurts. Not my head, which hit the concrete and should be throbbing.

My heart.

As they wheel me into the emergency room, I start to cry, and one of the nurse's pats my arm as she takes the IV bag away from the paramedics.

"Don't worry, sweetie. We'll have a look at that baby of yours, make sure he's okay."

"She," I correct her. But what I want to say is that I don't care about the stupid baby right now. Jeremiah's baby. I just want my old life back. I start crying harder. And it's so useless and frustrating because it's not like crying is going to make it happen. But I can't help it.

"Oh," she says, "I'm sorry." She wheels me into a curtained off area. "I'm sure she's just beautiful." Then she abruptly changes subjects and launches into the questions on the clipboard she's holding. Name… age… that gets an eyebrow raise.

"Are you sexually active?"

I glare and gesture out my belly. "Obviously." Not anymore though. Not for a while.

"Date of your last period?"

"Early August." I'm so sick of answering the same questions.

She nods and jots it down. Then she lowers her chart and looks me in the eye. "Do you feel safe at home?" That's a new one.

"What kind of question is that?"

"We have to ask it."

"Yes."

"Do you live with your boyfriend?"

Another tear escapes. "I don't have a boyfriend." Saying it aloud makes it feel so real. "I live with my mom." I think… I hope… If she'll take me. More tears build up and I stare at the ceiling, willing them to stay put.

"Do you want us to call your mom and let her know you're here?"

I nod, but I don't trust my voice to speak.

She clicks her pen and hangs the chart on the end of my bed. "The doctor will be in to see you soon."

* * *

I zone out while the doctors and nurses run tests. They draw blood, they shine lights into my eyes, they run a thermometer over my forehead, and through it all, I just stare at the wall in front of me. All of my emotions ran out of me earlier, now I'm just left with this void. And in it, I think about Granny.

Granny, who taught me that the Earth is a mother. The ocean, and the moon her daughters. That all of nature is a balance between Man and Woman. The balance between Jeremiah and me has been broken. I can feel that now. It's been broken for a long time, maybe ever since I got pregnant.

I'm not sure it can be repaired, and I don't think I want it to be.

There is a cycle for everything. For life and death, for love. I rub my belly, even for this. The cycle of Jeremiah and me is over. I have bigger things to care about now.

***

Mom arrives in full force just as the nurse is taking my blood pressure for what feels like the billionth time since I got there. That reading is probably blown, because my heart rate skyrockets as soon as she storms into the room.

"Dani!" she cries, rushing over to me and cupping my face with her hands. "I've been so worried! You just left, and I didn't know where you were. Then the hospital called." She pulls my head closer to kiss my forehead. "Thank God you're okay."

All the emotions I thought I had run out of start bubbling back. "Mom…" I manage to choke out before bawling.

She wraps her arms around my neck, pressing my face into her chest and combing her fingers through my hair. "Shhh… baby, it's okay. It's okay."

"I'm sorry…"

"You didn't do anything wrong, Dani." She leans back to look me in the eye. "You didn't do anything wrong."

Then it all comes pouring out of me. How I found Jeremiah and Shelby together, how I've been so angry at Dad for pushing me away when I needed him the most, how scared I've been all year, and how I've spent my whole life feeling like I've never been good enough for her.

"Dani," she says, staring me straight in the eye. "You're more than good enough for me. You're the most important person in my life. You'll always be better than perfect in my eyes."

My lower lip shakes, and I take two or three quick breaths. "Really?"

"Of course."

Waning Gibbous

Mom's story.

I feel like I've been waiting my entire life to hear Mom's side of the story. To hear the truth about her and Dad and Caleb. She doesn't waste any time. When I'm discharged from the hospital, the first thing she does is fix a mug of hot chocolate for me, tea for her, then she sits next to me on the sofa. Right next to me, so the weight and heat of her body press against me. She is so close to me, but her eyes are far away. They see something no one else can see.

"The months after you were born were so hard." She shakes her head. "I can't always put it into words what it's like. Well, you'll see. In a few weeks. You'll see. The way pregnancy destroys you while giving you everything.

"You spend nine months building up hormones in your body, for the sole purpose of creating life, then in a few short, painful hours, everything changes. After Caleb was born, all I felt was joy. Exhaustion, but joy. Unbridled, overwhelming joy.

"After you," she sighs, "not joy. Quite the opposite, in fact."

I can't take my eyes off her lips. They tremble, and she lifts her mug to drink, but her hands shake and hot tea spills onto her shirt. She sucks in a quick breath, and I grab the box of tissues on the table in front of us.

She continues as she dabs absentmindedly at the stain. "Everything about you was so hard, right from the beginning. It wasn't your fault. You were just a baby, but I wasn't used to the crying. Caleb had been easier. He hardly every cried. But you, I couldn't get you to stop. And your father," she snorts, "well, let's just say he was finding more and more excuses to escape the house."

"By the end of November, you were six months old, and I was at the end of my rope. I never had a moment to myself. As soon as you were down, your brother demanded my attention. He couldn't understand why his mommy who had laughed and played with him for four years of his life could now barely muster the energy to stand. On good days, I could manage. On bad, I barely left the sofa. Now, it's so obvious. I had post-partum depression. Plain and simple. But at the time... I didn't know, or I was in denial, or..."

I can't imagine my mom, the woman who out-does Pinterest in everything, lying around on a sofa all day, too depressed to do anything.

"And, I started drinking." She sips her tea. "It took the edge off. Your crying bothered me less. I was able to play with Caleb more. But it got worse.

"Your father suggested we go to Maine to visit his family for Christmas. At first, I made every excuse not to go, but your dad said his family would watch the kids. He told me I would get a break. I don't know. Maybe I was stupid. Maybe I thought we'd be able to get away, just the two of us, find a way back to each other. Maybe I thought if I could win him back, then the children would be easier."

She sighs. "Well, I was wrong. Being in Maine was harder than being home. His sisters had children of their own, and his parents were always busy. Every day became an obligation, another family outing through which I would have to smile and laugh and pretend I wasn't ready to implode at any moment.

"I don't even remember how it happened. Your dad was out with some old high school friends. His family was out doing something, and I was alone with just you and Caleb. And you. Oh the crying. I thought by six months, you would have outgrown it, but no. You hadn't. You cried and cried, and nothing I could do helped. I walked around the house a dozen times. I rocked. I sang every song I could think of. And you kept crying.

"And through it all, Caleb yanking on my leg, demanding to be played with, begging to go outside in the snow. It was so new to him. Exciting. He had never seen snow before." Mom stops speaking and pinches her eyes shut for a second. A tear slides down her cheek. "Then, I snapped." Her voice shakes. "I told him to just go. I wasn't thinking. I just needed him to leave me alone. Then I put you in your crib and let you scream while I hid in the bathroom with a bottle of wine."

She covers her mouth with her hand to stifle the sobs that are building up. "Your grandparents came home two hours later, and I was passed out on the bathroom floor. You were safe in your crib, but they couldn't find Caleb. We looked and looked, but we couldn't find him." Her voice cracks. "When we finally found him… in the woods behind their house… his lips were so blue. Even now, when I close my eyes, all I see are those blue lips. His beautiful lips."

She doubles over, sobbing, and I wrap my arms around her. "Mom, it's okay."

"It was my fault."

I don't think there's anything more terrifying for a kid to see then their own mom lose control. And that's what's happening right now. My mom has gone from the self-assured Super Mom to a woman undone by grief in just a few short minutes. And I'm stuck on the outside, watching helplessly.

Suddenly it's all so clear. Why Mom is the way she is. The overbearing nature, the involvement in every little thing. She's trying to prove she's not a failure. She's trying to prove that she is a good mom, that the worst moment of her life, one horrible incident, that it doesn't define her. Like she thinks if she just keeps busy enough, if she does everything exactly right, that maybe the Universe will forgive her for Caleb.

But maybe she doesn't need the Universe to forgive her. Maybe she just needs me.

"Mom?" I whisper.

She straightens up, dabs her eyes delicately with her tissue, then looks at me.

I swallow my fear and my pride and the lump in my throat. "I love you."

Maybe I've been avoiding Mom's eyes so long that I've forgotten what they look like, but I swear I see in their depths a glimmer of something akin to hope. She reaches up a hand and cups my cheek. "Oh Dani. I love you too.

My beautiful little girl."

Mom glosses over the rest of the story. The police investigation, the ultimate decision that it was an unfortunate accident. The time she spent in a mental health clinic a couple of towns over while Granny took care of me.

I don't need to hear about how hard she fought to get better, to get back to me. I already know.

Waning Gibbous

The next day, I have to go in to see Dr. Henderson because of the fall. It seems like the visit lasts forever, just to be told that I need to take it easy for a couple of weeks.

"Take it easy as in… I don't have to go to school?" I ask hopefully. Mom sighs in the background.

Dr. Henderson looks at me. "I suppose it wouldn't be the worst thing in the world for you to take a few days off. Give your body a chance to heal from your tumble."

I glance gleefully at Mom, but she shakes her head ruefully. "You still have to keep up with your schoolwork."

"I know."

"Fine," she concedes. "You can take a few days off and see how you feel."

How I feel is amazing, because I plan on using those few days to convince Mom to enroll me in the online home-schooling program. I figure if I really push myself, I might even be able to graduate by December. Something tells me going back to school in August isn't going to be easy with a four-month-old baby to take care of. But if I could work from home, maybe it wouldn't be so bad.

It's a long shot, but I have to try. Especially since the idea of seeing Shelby in the halls is horrifying. I still haven't gotten the image of her and Jeremiah out of my head. I'm not even sure where Jer and I stand, except wherever it is, it seems like we're on opposite corners of the room. And I don't even know how it happened. In my heart, I still love him, but I also hate him. And I start to wonder if the love I feel is more like nostalgia. For that part of my life which seems completely gone now.

New Moon

It is official. Danielle Miller is no longer enrolled at James Polk High School. Homeschooling, here I come.

Okay, it's not official yet. Mom's in the principal's office signing the paperwork as we speak, but any second now, I'll be free.

I thought I'd have to really fight with Mom to get her to agree, but it was actually surprisingly simple. I just put all my research in front of her, told her my plan to graduate early, and she just nodded and said she trusted me.

It's like I have a whole new mom.

Of course, I didn't expect that she'd drag me back up to the building to file all the necessary paperwork. I had been kind of hoping I would never have to see the place ever again. Or anyone in it.

Luckily, no one ever hangs out in the principal's office.

I spend my time playing on my phone, that is until the door swings open and in strolls Mr. Craig. He drops a paper off with the secretary, but his eyes never leave my seat, and as soon as he's done with all his own work, he walks over to me.

"Danielle, how have you been?"

"Fine."

"Are you coming back to class? We've really missed you."

I shake my head. "I'm actually unenrolling. I'm going to be homeschooled. Do the coursework online. I want to try to graduate early if I can."

His face looks sad and happy at the same time, I have no idea how to read it. "I know you can do it. You're a very talented young lady." He jerks his head toward the door. "Do you mind coming back to my classroom for a bit? I want to give you something before you leave."

I glance to where my mom is still sitting behind closed doors with the principal. "I guess."

Mr. Craig glances toward the secretary. "Mrs. Thomas, can you let Danielle's mother know where she is?"

A quick nod from the woman, and we're off.

Mr. Craig slows his pace so I can keep up with him, even though I can tell it's killing him. His usual high-energy power-walking self can't stand the pregnant waddle.

"I was worried when I found out you had been in the hospital. Everyone in homeroom was pretty shaken up."

Everyone, sure. I bet Shelby had a really hard time with it. "It was really stupid. I just slipped on some stairs."

"Yes, well, I'm glad you're okay." He stops in front of his classroom and opens the door, letting me in first. Then, he rummages around in his desk while I look around. Nothing has changed. The same posters on the walls, the same student work on the bulletin board. It's the exact same classroom, but it feels so different. Smaller.

"Here," he says, "you should take this."

He holds my Creative Writing journal out to me.

"Thanks," I say, grabbing it.

"And I want you to promise to keep writing," he says, "I know it'll be hard to find the time. Trust me, I know. But even if you just put down a few lines a day, anything. Keep at it. Your voice is important."

I nod, this time the "thanks" is a little harder to get out.

"Great," he says, "Well, I gotta run, but I'm really glad I had a chance to talk to you, one last time, Danielle."

He's halfway out the door but I stop him. "Mr. Craig?"

He pokes his head back in. "Yes?"

"Why do you call me Danielle? Everyone always calls me Dani."

Mr. Craig smiles. "Don't you think the time for Dani is over? You're a whole new person these days."

Then he's gone, leaving me alone in his classroom. I start to follow, but something stops me. This is crazy, completely insane, but I can't leave this place without leaving my mark on it somehow. Even something little. Insignificant.

I grab a permanent marker from his desk, and take it back to my own seat where I spent the entire school year. With some effort, and a lot of discomfort, I crawl underneath and write on the underside of the desk:

Dani was [x]
Maybe you didn't notice
You might not be aware
Dani was [x]
She once walked these halls
For who knows for how long?
Kind of a nobody
Invisible
Now she's gone.
But Dani was [x]
It's easy to forget
Really
No one will blame you if you do
But I swear
Dani was [x]

First Quarter

"What would you like for your birthday, this year?" Mom springs the question on me before I've completely woken up. I haven't even had my first bite of breakfast.

"For this baby to get out of my body," I grumble.

"I don't think I'll be able to swing that, anything else?"

"For Jer to not have cheated on me."

"Try again."

I look up and see she's smiling. At least she has a sense of humor about this. "You know what would be really cool?"

She shakes her head no. "Enlighten me."

"If we could somehow convince the staff at Granny's home to let us take her to the beach with us. Just for an afternoon." I close my eyes. "Granny loves the beach."

"Yes, she does."

"I mean, if you think it'd be okay..." I backtrack. I don't want Mom to think I have my hopes set on this. It really just came to me. But it'd be perfect. One last big outing, just the three of us, before the baby comes. And the weather is finally warm enough we could probably roll our pants up and walk around barefoot in the shallows. I can already feel it, the wet sand giving way beneath my toes, the splash of water as it rolls over my ankles.

Mom dashes all those hopes though. "You're too close to your due date to be traveling out of town, honey."

My face falls.

"We can try after the baby is born," she adds.

"How long would we have to wait? How old does she have to be?"

Mom shrugs. "Not long. Just a few months. We'll take care of her. The ocean is in her blood, after all."

I can't wait to take the baby to the beach for the first time. I can already imagine it, the look in her eyes when she sees the vast expanse of water for the first time. There's nothing better. It's as good an offer as I'm going to get, so I nod.

"I'll talk to the nursing home, see if we can bring Granny along."

"Okay." I finish eating, then head up to my room. "I have some more homework to do."

Now that I'm officially homeschooled, I have complete control over my education. And it's perfect. I actually get more done working at my own pace than I ever did at school. Even Mom agrees it's been better for me.

My goal is to power through all of my Junior year courses before the baby arrives, which means I'm working doubly hard on everything. But it also means I have to do the math and science stuff on my own. I try to get through a chapter a week on each of those, but it's hard. The literature work is easier. I'm a natural at those. I do it all online, and some invisible teacher somewhere grades my essays and emails them back to me.

I can work on my own time. Which is great. I get a lot done in the mornings, then about one o'clock, I crash. I can't help it. I'm just too exhausted to think anymore. Then I can wake up a couple hours later and get some more work done. No way I could have gotten away with a nap in the middle of the school day before, but I'm actually more productive this way.

It's Saturday, so I think Mom thought I was a little crazy when I said I wanted to get some homework done, but I think I can probably get through my Algebra II final this week if I keep pushing.

I'm about halfway through with taking notes off the online video and about to start the assignment when my phone rings. I glance at the screen. It's Jeremiah.

I let it ring three more times before picking up. "Hello?"

"Hey, Dani… it's me."

"Yeah."

"I was wondering if we could talk?" He sighs into the phone. "Is this a good time?"

Is there ever a good time for this kind of talk? "I guess."

"Well, it's just that, I guess I think we've been trying to hold onto something that really isn't there anymore." He's been practicing. I can hear it in his voice. Good, I think. I like that he was nervous. He should be nervous. He cheated on his pregnant girlfriend. He keeps talking, "Like, I mean, I still love you and all."

I roll my eyes.

"But," he says, "I just don't think this is going to work out. Trying to stick together, just for the baby."

"Yeah."

"I mean, I still want to be there for it, I mean her. But I just don't think I want to be with you."

"Yeah," I mutter. I stare at my computer screen.

"Is that all you're going to say?" he asks.

I nod, even though he can't see it. "Yeah." Then I hang up.

Enough is enough. What's the point of prolonging the inevitable? I knew from the second I saw that pregnancy test all those months ago, that Jeremiah would run for the hills. It just took him a lot longer to do it. I should give him credit for that. For sticking around as long as he did.

And it's great he wants to be there for the baby, but I'm not stupid. I know that's just talk. He'll go off to MIT, get his fancy degree, and start a job who knows where doing who knows what? I lean back and rub my stomach, and the baby gives a thump in response.

Then I notice all the pictures of Jeremiah taped to my wall. Time for a change.

I grab my little trash can and walk around the room, pulling pictures down. Pictures of us kissing at a Tae Kwon Do tournament, of us dancing at Homecoming, of Jeremiah carrying me piggy-back. All of them go into the trash. When I'm done, I pull the ultrasound pictures out of my desk drawer, find my favorite one with my baby's perfect little button nose in profile, and tape it to the empty space above my bed.

That's better.

Sometimes, I think we women do a little bit better without the men in our lives always messing things up. Between my mom and my Granny, this girl's going to have some amazing women to look up to.

Maybe losing Jeremiah isn't such a bad thing.

Waning Gibbous

I've officially started working at Earth's Bounty with Mom. It's part of our agreement. I can do online school until I finish my high school degree, but I have to work part time at her office. Doing the most boring of boring jobs… filing.

"What about after the baby is born?" I ask. It should be any day now. I am officially "full term" according to Dr. Henderson. It can't happen a moment too soon. I feel like I could pop at any second. But every time I complain, Mom reminds me that the longer the baby stays put, the healthier she'll be.

"After the baby is born," Mom says glibly, "we'll figure it out. You'll need some time to recuperate, but I'll bet you get antsy and start begging to leave the house before too long. And when that happens…" she sets a stack of papers to file in front of me, "your job will be waiting for you. The baby can sleep in my office in a pop-up crib."

Sheesh. She's worked everything out. There's no escape.

As soon as I've done all the busy work she can find me, I settle down in her office with my laptop, a pair of headphones, and my math textbook. I manage to power through a couple assignments, before my mind starts to wander, and I open up a blank word document.

I type: *Before You Enter This World*

Then I sit and stare at the screen.

Before you enter this world, daughter,
Here are some things you should know.
Your father and I loved each other,

Then we didn't.
Your grandmother and I hated each other,
Then we didn't.
There will be times when you and I love each other,
Then we won't
Then we will again.
Because that's what family is all about.
But know, dearest one, that my love for you started before you took your first
breath,
Before you opened your eyes.
Before we saw each other for the first time.
My heart has been beating in your ears for months,
And it will continue beating for you until my last breath.
All for you.
Just as my mother's beat for me.
And her mother's for her.
And every mother before that.
Before you enter this world, daughter.
Some things you should know.
The Women of your life are strong
And fierce
And independent
And you will be, too.
I know it.
Because you are my daughter.
My mother's granddaughter.
And my Granny's great granddaughter.
It's in your blood.

I stop typing and wipe the tears from my cheeks. Then, I click the save button and minimize the document.

New Moon

Friendship is laughing over shared jokes
Loaning someone a few bucks when they forget their lunch.
Being ready with chocolate ice cream and sappy movies after a bad breakup.
It is not dishonest or cruel.
It doesn't stab you in the back.
Make fun of you.
Steal something you love.
Friendship is a thousand things,
But it's not this.
And it's not you.

Shelby comes by the house the first week of May. Totally out of the blue. We haven't spoken since my fall. If I'm honest with myself, it's been kind of awesome.

When Mom knocks on my bedroom door, I tell her I don't want to talk to Shelby, but she says it might make me feel better, and at any rate, I need closure, so eventually, I let her in.

"Hey, Dani," she says, poking her head around my door.

I give a half-hearted grunt which she takes to mean "come on in," because she does.

"Look, I just wanted to apologize."

I glue my eyes to my laptop screen, refusing to look at her. "Not accepted."

"Because," she continues, "I really messed up. And it was all my fault. I mean, I came onto him, okay? So you can stop being mad at Jer."

"Great," I snap, "Thanks for clarifying that you seduced my ex-boyfriend. Love the visual."

I sneak a glance, just in time to see her shrink in on herself.

"He's really broken up about it. Thinks you never want to see him again."

"I don't," I say, "but I have to. Over and over again for the rest of my life. I will always have to see him and remember what he did. But you? I don't have to see you."

Her head snaps up. "So that's it? We're not friends anymore?"

I force myself to make eye contact. "Honestly, Shelby? I'm not sure we were ever friends."

"What do you mean?"

"Oh, I don't know. Just that this year has been incredibly hard for me, and it would have been nice to be able to rely on my best friend for support. But what did I really get from you? You guilt tripped me about not getting rid of the baby, you made fun of me behind my back to anyone who would listen. You spent the entire year bringing me down. Then, you made out with my boyfriend, and I don't even understand why."

"Dani—" she starts, but I cut her off.

"And it hasn't even been just this year. You know what I realized, Shelby? You're a mean person. For as long as I've known you, you've turned everyone else's struggle into your own personal joke. I'm sick of it. I don't need you anymore. And I don't want you around my daughter."

For a while, Shelby sits on my bed staring at her lap. Long enough for me to wonder whether I should tell her to leave. Then she clears her throat. "I don't have any other friends besides you." Her voice cracks, and I see a tear on her cheek which rolls down and falls onto her folded hands.

"Then, I guess you don't have any friends," I say.

Never in my life have I stood up for myself like this. I've always let Jeremiah or Shelby take over in difficult social settings. But now I've rid myself of both of them, and I feel...

Strong.

Full Moon

The contractions start at night, and they are just like Mom said they would be, like period cramps. At first, I don't even notice them. I just wake up feeling sore but not knowing why. Then I realize what's going on. Cramp, then release. Wait several minutes. Cramp, then release.

Contractions.

I climb out of bed and plod across the hall to Mom's room, but she's already awake.

"Everything okay, honey?" she asks as she sits up and grabs her glasses off the night stand.

I nod and stand in front of her, huge pregnant me. "I think it's starting."

She stretches dramatically, then grabs her phone, unlocking it to start an app. "Let me know when the next one starts."

"What's that?" I ask.

"It tracks of contractions, the timing and duration. That way we'll know when to start heading to the hospital."

My mom, she thinks of everything. She must have known I'd be too scatterbrained to think about it on my own.

"What time is it?" I ask.

"About three in the morning."

"Ugh," I groan, "Why couldn't this stupid baby come at a normal time?"

"They never come at normal times," she says. "Think you can go back to sleep for a little? You'll need your rest."

"No."

"Okay." Mom climbs out of bed and gives another big stretch. "Then I guess we're up. Want something to eat?"

I wrinkle my nose. Who can think of eating at this time?

She must have read my mind. "They're not going to let you eat once they check you into the hospital."

"Really? Why not?"

She shrugs. "It's just the rules. If I were you, I'd try to get something in your stomach. You don't know how long this could last."

"Okay, okay," I say, following her down the hallway toward the stairs.

"What sounds good?"

"I dunno, whatever."

"I'm in the mood for waffles. How about that?"

As soon as she says it, it sounds perfect. "Yes."

"Waffles it is."

Nothing happens while she breaks the egg into the bowl and whisks in the flour and sugar. Nothing happens while she's pouring the first batch into the waffle iron. But as she lifts the steaming pastry out, I can feel another contraction rolling in.

I wince. "Got one."

"Oh." She scrambles for her phone and presses the start button. "Let me know when it's over. And breathe."

I do what she says, breathing for several seconds, then say, "Okay, it's done."

"Twenty-seven seconds. Not bad. Once they're about five minutes apart, we'll go to the hospital." Then, as if nothing happened, she slides the plate toward me, steam rising off the golden waffle.

* * *

I expected labor to last like a few hours tops. I kind of thought when the baby woke me up at three in the morning, I'd be in the hospital pushing her out by noon. I did not expect to be spending the day lying on the sofa counting the minutes between contractions and wondering why they're not progressing faster.

By four in the afternoon, I'm bored out of my mind. The intermittent pain means I can't focus on a book or homework. Even phone games have lost their joy. "How long between those?" I ask as another contraction ebbs.

"Seven minutes," mom replies, not looking up from her phone.

"This is taking forever."

"Babies move at their own pace, Dani."

"Well why won't this one move faster?"

She shrugs.

"That is so not helpful."

"Let's go for a walk."

"A walk?" I complain, "my body is trying to kill me right now, and you want to go for a walk?"

"Sometimes it helps move things along."

That is all the motivation I need. I heave myself off of the sofa. "Let me get my shoes on."

Mom waits patiently in the foyer as I slide my shoes on. Slip-ons, still, because of the huge stomach. Then, she hands me my jacket. Because apparently, she is still going to baby me, even when I'm on the verge of becoming a mom.

Oh my God. I'm becoming a mom today. Or tomorrow, depending on how slow this little girl wants to be.

I yank the jacket on begrudgingly. "Okay, let's go."

Mom leads the way, but when we get to the sidewalk, she stops. "You set the pace."

I'm pretty slow. I guess my daughter and I have that in common. Even when I wasn't pregnant, I liked to take my time. But now that I'm huge and clumsy, well, we basically crawl down the street. We make it about halfway down the block before the next contraction comes on, and I stop walking and grab Mom's arm.

She has her phone app open in record time, all the while reminding me to breathe.

I try to take long low breaths, like they told us to in birthing class, but I end up just wincing and groaning in pain. "Please tell me we can go to the hospital now."

"Not yet, I'm sorry."

"Ugh."

"So," Mom says, "have you told Jeremiah you're in labor yet?"

"Wow, talk about a change in subject." I glance at her. "No, not yet."

"Don't you think you should?"

Yes, obviously. But Jer and I haven't spoken since the whole break up. Still, it's the right thing to do. I pull my phone out of my pocket and press the speed dial. He's still my number one speed dial. Eventually, I'll have to change that.

I hold my breath while it rings, secretly praying he doesn't pick up.

No such luck.

"Hello? Dani?" Is that a hint of hope in his voice?

"Hey."

"Is everything okay?"

"Yeah, just, well I guess I'm in labor."

Mom snorts in the background.

"You guess?"

"Well, I've been having contractions since 3 am."

"And you're just now telling me?" Hard to ignore the familiar sound of disappointment in his voice.

"Yeah."

"So, should I meet you at the hospital?"

"I'm not there yet."

"Why not?"

"Well, Jeremiah," I say, putting on my bossiest, most Mom-like, nagging voice, "if you had bothered to attend the birthing classes with me like I asked you to, you would know that you're not supposed to go to the hospital until the contractions are about five minutes apart. And they're at seven right now."

"Okay, okay!" he groans, "Just text me when you're heading up there."

"Fine."

"Okay."

"Bye." I hang up before he can say "bye" back to me and turn to glare at Mom.

"So," Mom says with a smirk, "things still difficult with him?"

"You think?" I start walking back toward the house. "Is it ever going to not be hard?"

She slides an arm around my shoulder as we walk. "It depends. Your dad and I never really got the whole separate parenting thing down."

No, they really didn't. Even now, they're at odds about everything to do with me.

"But," she continues, "you and Jer might be different. You don't have the same…" her voice trails away.

"Heartbreak," I offer. She means we don't have the looming pain of a lost child in our past. We're still relatively undamaged by the world.

"Yeah," she agrees.

I lean my head on her shoulder while we walk.

* * *

I end up staying home until about eight. By then, the contractions are getting closer together and I can barely breathe through the pain. Mom makes the final decisions. She grabs my overnight bag and my jacket and leads me to the door. "C'mon, baby. It's time."

My hands shake as I text Jeremiah from the passenger seat in my mom's car. I can't even pay attention to the street signs as they flit past. All I can think about is the steadily growing pain in my back and abdomen, no longer like period cramps but so much worse.

Suddenly, I feel all too aware that this is happening. Right now.

And I think that all of pregnancy has been like the first hill on a roller coaster. That steady climb to the top. It drags on forever. Then finally, you're at the top, and you peer over the edge. And the hill looks too big, too terrifying. The roller coaster stops, waiting for the drop, and you think, just for half a second, that maybe you shouldn't have ever gotten on in the first place.

That maybe you would have been happier on the ground. But it's too late, you can't get off now.

Another contraction rolls in, and I moan.

"We're almost there, baby. Just try to breathe."

"It hurts."

"I know. I know."

We pull into the hospital parking lot, and Mom leaps from the car as soon as the engine dies. She scampers around to my side and helps me out, looping her arm around my waist as we trudge to the entrance. "Almost there."

Once we get inside, we have to fill out paperwork. The woman who sits at reception doesn't bat an eye as I groan and rub my stomach. "Are you sure you're in labor?" she asks, and I glare.

"Pretty sure," I snap.

"How far apart are the contractions?"

Mom answers for me. "Four minutes."

She nods and slides over a handful of forms. "Fill these out, and we'll wheel you back in just a sec."

"Just a sec" stretches into seven minutes, during which I get two more contractions. Jeremiah shows up just in time for the second one, with his mom hot on his heels. He starts to make his way toward me, then pauses, as if unsure. By the time he makes up his mind to sit down next to me, the contraction has already subsided.

I relax against the back of the waiting room chair with a sigh.

"How are you feeling?" he asks.

"Like I'm about to push a human being out of my vagina," I snap. "You?"

He doesn't answer. Smart move.

The nurse walks back into the waiting room. "Danielle Miller?"

I struggle to my feet, and Jeremiah pops up after me. There's an awkward moment when both he and my mom start for the heavy locking doors between the waiting room, and the hallway full of delivery rooms, then they both stop and look at me.

The nurse looks up from her clipboard. "Are both of them joining you?" I'm allowed two people in the delivery room. I only want one.

I shake my head. "Just my mom."

Full Moon

I'm not going to go into the nitty-gritty details of having a baby. It hurts. Really bad. And basically everyone under the sun got a good look at my lady parts tonight. Enough that I'm not even all that embarrassed anymore. I guess that's just part of the game.

Around nine o'clock, the anesthesiologist shows up to put in the epidural, which I freak out about, naturally. It's not every day I have to sit still and let someone insert a needle into my spine. The only reason I agree to it is because the contractions are coming right on top of each other and I don't think I can stand it anymore. Mom holds my hands the entire time, and keeps whispering in my ear to just keep breathing, so I do, and then, sweet relief.

My body's been in pain so long, I almost don't even recognize the feeling of being pain free. I relax immediately. All the muscles in my arms and legs, even my neck, that have been tensing through each contraction finally release and I feel like I can breathe again. Finally.

Mom kisses my forehead and helps me lie back down. "There now, try to get some rest. You'll need your strength for when it's time to push."

I nod and lean my head back on my pillow. Even though the epidural has taken away the pain, I can still feel the muscles tightening and relaxing, tightening and relaxing. I swallow the lump in my throat. "I can't do it, Mom."

"Yes, you can." She settles into the chair next to me and brushes my hair off my forehead. "You can, and you will, because, quite frankly, you don't have a choice."

I turn my face to look at her.

"How are you feeling?" she whispers.

"Really scared."

"That's normal." Then she gives my hand a squeeze. "But I'll be right here with you the entire time. I won't leave your side. I promise."

* * *

Around ten thirty, my stomach churns, then I throw up all over myself. The nurse doesn't even bat an eye. "Oh good," she says as she helps me out of my dirty gown. "That means you're close."

"Great," I groan.

She's right. Less than fifteen minutes later, she says I need to start pushing. Dr. Henderson pops her head into the room for the first time all evening. Another interesting fact about the delivery room, the nurses do all the work. Seriously.

Even though I'm medicated, and I can't feel the pain, the pushing is still hard. So hard. I push with all my strength, and I feel like nothing is happening, but Mom rubs my back and tells me I'm doing a good job. The nurse tells me to look down, and I chance a glance, even though I know it's going to be disgusting, and I see a head. An actual head.

I don't know. Maybe I thought it wasn't really happening. But that's when it hits me.

"One more big push, Dani," Dr. Henderson says, and as the contraction comes on, I bear down as hard as I can, grunting loudly then...

She's born.

She's alive.

She's... getting her umbilical cord clipped and being handed to me, all naked and slimy and all I can think to say through the entire thing is, "oh my God, oh my God, oh my God."

Because I just had a baby.

A real, live, human baby.

Oh my God.

I start crying. I can't help it. I don't understand why. I'm not sad. Not in the least. I'm happy. Happier than I've ever been in my entire life. I pull her closer and examine every inch of her. Peach fuzz covers her head, not really hair, but close, one nose, two eyes that are still closed to the world, and a mouth that opens and shuts, opens and shuts. Two arms curled up against her chest, and two long legs. She's so beautiful, I'm sure my heart is actually going to explode.

"Oh my God," I keep repeating. "Oh my God." I'm a broken record when it comes to this giving birth thing.

At some point, the nurse takes her away to be measured, weighed, cleaned. All those things that have to happen, but my body yearns for her to return, like it's never wanted anything before. I can't stop looking at her, and even though she's only a few feet away, it feels like a thousand miles, because I can't get up and go to her.

She's only gone a minute, then they bring her back, wrapped in a towel, and place her in my arms. Where she belongs.

* * *

Jeremiah has to wait another couple of hours before they let him in to see us. There are a ton of medical things I need to go through first. Like surviving the humiliation of my first post-baby pee. Eventually, though, the baby and I are settled into our hospital room, cleaned as well as we're going to be and ready for a visitor.

Jeremiah peeks his head around the corner. "Are you decent?"

I roll my eyes. "You've seen me naked, Jer."

"Yeah, but..." he blushes. "I don't know."

"I'm decent. As decent as I can get, considering." I gesture for him to come inside. "Don't you want to meet your daughter?"

He grins and scampers in. "Yeah."

I cradle our baby in my arms one last time, then lean forward to hand her off to him. His eyes widen. "She's so tiny."

I laugh. "Seven pounds, eight ounces. So pretty average, actually."

"She's…" he sighs. He can't finish the sentence. I swear, I can see tears in his eyes.

I know the feeling. "Yeah."

He leans down and grazes a kiss on her forehead. And for a second, I think I see my Jeremiah in those lips, but he's not mine anymore. He's hers. It's a sacrifice I'm willing to make.

"What do you want to name her?" he asks.

"Evelyn," I reply automatically. I've been thinking about it for weeks, and I'm not backing down. "After my grandmother. And Hannah for a middle name."

"After your mom," he finishes for me. "I like it."

"Really?" I'm a little shocked he's not arguing for his own ideas.

He nods and hands Evelyn back to me. "She's your daughter, Dani. You did everything for her. You deserve to name her."

Epilogue

Mom sits on the sofa next to me where I feed a four-month old Evie, and says simply, "next Thursday."

"Next Thursday, what?"

"Next Thursday, you, me, Evie, and your grandmother are driving out to Langley Beach." She gives my hand a squeeze. "Belated birthday present." She must have pulled about a thousand strings to make this happen.

My heart leaps to my throat. "Really?"

"Yes, really. There are rules, of course. But mainly we have to have Granny back by evening check in. Eight pm."

"We can have the whole day?" I gasp. It's almost too much.

"We better make it count."

* * *

The weather could not be more beautiful if it tried. It's like all of Mother Nature has gathered together and promised me this perfect day. A day with all the Roth women from Granny down to little Evelyn.

I spend all morning packing our bags. Sandwiches for lunch, blankets to lay out on, some towels in case we get wet, sunscreen, and bottled breastmilk for Evie, because I'm still not sure about feeding in public. Mom says it's perfectly natural, but I feel so exposed. Everything. I check again and again, because it has to be perfect.

On the way there, I sit in the backseat petting Evie's downy brown hair and making funny faces while she giggles and spits bubbles. Granny hums to herself as she smiles at the trees rushing past. We roll the windows down and let the sun shine on our faces, the wind dance through our hair. When

Granny smiles, I see a little of her old self. The Granny I knew before the Alzheimer's. Sometimes I think what she really needs, more than medication and constant surveillance, are days like this. Freedom and the feeling of fresh air in her lungs.

But, I know it's not safe for her. Not recently. Mom and I had to sign a dozen papers swearing we will keep a close eye on every movement she makes, and bring her right back at the first sign of trouble.

There won't be trouble though. I can feel it in my bones. This day is my day. Our day.

It's late enough in the season that the beach is fairly empty. The tourists mostly come in the summer, when the heat and the crowd make it impossible to enjoy anyway. This is the best time. When the air is still warm, but the beach deserted. The shallow water that plays on the sand, dancing up the bank, then rushing back down has been heated by the sun.

I don't waste a second. As soon as the blankets have been thrown down, and the cooler dug into the sand, Evelyn safely strapped into her bouncy chair beneath a broad umbrella, I yank my sandals off and roll my pants up to my knees then rush out to the water to play. For a split second, I forget about the past year. After months of exhaustion, the sea air breathes new life into me. I am a child again. Happy and carefree.

Granny laughs in the background. "That girl was born under a water sign."

Then, I hear Mom's sigh of annoyance. Because I wasn't, and the old Granny knew that. I may as well have been. The water calls to me.

I wade up to my knees and run my fingers through the brine. The wet sand gives way between my toes, and I sink. I long to throw my arms wide and fall into the water, to let it buoy me along. But behind me, my daughter coos for me, instinct kicks in, and I return to her.

I lift her into the air, delighting in her giggles until Mom reminds me her skin is delicate and must be slathered in sunscreen.

"I want her to see the water."

"And she will," Mom says, "After you put sunscreen on her, and a hat. And eat something."

There's no sense in arguing, and besides, she's right. I'm starving.

We eat our lunches as the sun peaks above us. I'm still learning to eat one-handed with Evelyn cradled in my arms. Still clumsy. Eventually, Mom takes pity on me and removes her from my arms to feed her a bottle of milk while I scarf down two whole sandwiches.

"I'm going to get fat if I keep eating like this," I complain.

Mom shakes her head and smiles down at Evie. "Your body needs the extra protein."

Right again.

We laze around in the sunshine, soaking in the warmth until our food has digested, then I strap Evelyn to my chest with one of those hands-free carriers. It feels so natural. Even though she is out here, breathing salty air all on her own, she still feels so much a part of me. Of my body. The four of us walk along the beach, splashing our toes in the shallows. I dip Evelyn in, and like her mother, she takes to it instantly, kicking her tiny legs with joy.

When the sun sinks behind our backs, and shadows start to fall over the sand, Mom sighs and checks her watch. "We should head home."

I know I should agree, but it feels too soon. Time has slipped past us too quickly, not so much that day, but all the days, the weeks and months that ran together to form this messed up year of mine.

And Granny has been more lucid in these few hours with us than she has been in a long time, and I suddenly hate that we have to take her back. I long to keep her home with us, all four of us.

I trudge back to the blankets and help Mom fold and pack them back into our bag. Until finally we're ready to go home.

Mom pauses, peering up at the footpath back to our car, then sighs. "I don't want to go."

"Me neither."

Granny slips her hand into mine, the other grasps Mom's, so the three of us stand shoulder to shoulder on the beach, none of us wanting to move but knowing we must.

"Maybe we could take a picture?" I offer. It's a silly suggestion, the idea that a picture could capture this. The beauty of this moment.

But Mom catches onto the idea and won't let it go. "Yes, let's!" And like a teenager with a group of friends, she pulls out her phone and wraps and arm around Granny's shoulders, pulling me close on the other side. "Smile."

I don't need to be told twice. This has been one of the best days of my life. I slide an arm around Granny's waist, the other pulling back Evie's wrap so her sleeping face is just visible, and smile at the selfie mode. A second later, we're all admiring the picture, probably one of the only times in my life I've taken a selfie and not immediately hated how I look.

Mom smiles. "Four generations of beautiful women."

Granny nods. "Daughters of the sea."

I caress Evie's hair. "Isn't she perfect?"

Mom reaches past Granny and tucks my hair behind my ear. "Yes, she is."

About the Author

Sarah is a high school teacher and mother of two whose short fiction has been published in several anthologies. Her contemporary YA novels and short fiction fiercely tackle the gamut of tough issues that affect real teenagers. You can find her in Kansas City with her two boys and her husband, where she's often crocheting, singing along with music that is entirely too loud, or snuggling with her cat, Osiris.

You can connect with me on:

🌐 https://sarahkaminskiauthor.wixsite.com/website

🔗 https://www.instagram.com/sarahkamwrites

Subscribe to my newsletter:

✉ https://mailchi.mp/2144bc9871ba/2ichfp7xkm

www.ingramcontent.com/pod-product-compliance
Lightning Source LLC
Chambersburg PA
CBHW060311310726
48976CB00007B/2292